The
Bold Ship
Phenomenal

To Kevin,
      The first in
   NZ.
        With love.
            Sarah.

For Ben and our four boys, all of whom know
where adventure is to be found – SJ

Published in 2015 by Flat Bed Press
PO Box 131, Raglan, New Zealand 3225

www.sarahjohnson.co.nz

Text © Sarah Johnson, 2015
Illustrations © Sarah Johnson, 2015

ISBN 978-0-473-31314-2

Cover illustration and artwork by Deborah Hinde: www.picturebook.co.nz
Edited by Sue Copsey: www.suecopsey.com
Typeset in Horley Old Style by Book Design Ltd: www.bookdesign.co.nz
Printed and bound in China by Asia Pacific Offset Ltd

The
Bold Ship
Phenomenal

SARAH JOHNSON

Chapter one

MALACHI FOUND THE BOTTLE on the shore.

He was kicking along the tide line when he saw it, each jab of his toe scattering the sand before him in a damp pink fan.

"Science sucks," he said, booting at the sand. "Science sucks, science s …"

Then he saw the bottle, and he stopped.

The bottle was propped on the edge of a shallow pool, scooped by the retreating sea. Further down the beach, the sea slid *ssshh ssshh* onto the sand, but the pool that the bottle rested in was perfectly still, cradling its glassy catch.

Normally this was the sort of thing that interested Malachi. Jetsam and flotsam: trinkets and treasures delivered by the sea. He would squirrel his findings home to consider in the peace of his room. Where had they come from? Whose had they been? Were they discarded, or lost?

This morning, though, he couldn't be bothered. Not after the way his day had kicked off. Malachi aimed another grumpy swipe at the sand and hoisted his bag up his back. He would have to hurry. Science was the first lesson of the day and he was already late.

Yet something about the bottle drew back his eye. Something about the way it reclined, half in, half out of the pool; as if it was struggling to stand upright, against the weight of whatever was inside.

With a sigh, Malachi dropped his bag and

walked down the beach to the pool's edge. He eased the bottle free. It was covered in sand, so he rinsed it in the pool.

The bottle was large and surprisingly heavy, with a long narrow neck and a bulbous belly that gave it an old-fashioned appearance. Stained string coiled around its neck, below a red wax-coated bung. Grey barnacles clung to its belly and base, and its glass was coated in slime and salt.

Malachi stretched his sleeve over his hand and dipped it in the pool. He rubbed the bottle with the wet sleeve, trying to make a clear space in the glass, so he could see inside.

As he rubbed, the sound of the ocean filled his head. Gently at first – *ssshh, ssshh, ssshh* – then building, until the waves' song thumped and thundered on the shore. Startled, Malachi looked up, but the beach was quiet; the small waves melting back into themselves before they'd finished their journey up the sand.

Malachi turned his attention back to the bottle. His rubbing had made no difference; the glass was still too murky to see inside. The bottle felt heavy, as if it might be full, but when he shook it, no liquid sloshed against the glass. He would have liked to have taken it home and cleaned it properly, but there was no time for that now.

He took off his jersey and wrapped it carefully around the bottle, before placing it in the top of his bag. Then, trying to keep as even a pace as possible, he jogged along the tide line, making up for lost time as he headed straight for school.

Chapter two

MALACHI HAD BEEN DREAMING when his father stuck his head around the bedroom door, earlier that morning.

"Come on lazybones, time to get up."

Malachi had scraped his duvet off his face. "What day is it?" he asked.

"Wednesday," said his father.

"Excellent!" Malachi sat up. "Only three days until the weekend."

"Have you got plans?" his father asked.

"We're going camping, remember?" said Malachi.

His father scratched his head. "Was that this weekend?"

He'd promised months ago that they would go camping this weekend. Malachi had wanted to go at the time, but his father had said things were still too unsettled after Mum, and Malachi hadn't felt able to argue. So they'd picked a weekend several months out, and Malachi had marked it on his calendar with a thick black cross.

"X marks the spot," he'd said, and he'd been looking forward to it ever since.

Now the weekend had finally arrived.

"I'll clean the tent after school," he'd said this morning. "It'll need it after all this time."

But his father had sighed. "I don't know, Malachi. I'd forgotten all about it."

"That doesn't matter, Dad. I can get the stuff together. I know where it all is."

"It's not that, Malachi," his father said. "It's just that I have so much to do here and I'm still really busy at work. I was hoping to make a start on the garden, it's turning into a jungle. Perhaps, you could help me with that instead?"

Malachi had stared at his father in disbelief. "But you promised. If Mum was here ..."

For a moment his father had looked like he might crumble. Then he'd straightened his tie and shaken his head. "I'm sorry, Malachi. I know you're disappointed, but that's just the way things are at the moment."

After that, there hadn't seemed much point in getting up, and when Malachi had finally rolled out of bed he was already late. Finding the bottle had made him later still, and by the time he reached school, the playing fields and courtyards were empty.

Through the science lab windows, he could see his classmates, already seated at their desks. Mrs Green was up the front, writing on the whiteboard. Malachi took a deep breath and pushed open the lab door. His day may have started off badly, but he had the distinct feeling it was about to get worse.

Chapter three

MRS GREEN PAUSED, pen poised mid-stroke, as Malachi scuttled towards his seat at the back.

Jarrod was already there, hunched over the bench. He ignored Malachi, as Malachi got out his pens and books. *Fine*, thought Malachi. He wasn't in the mood for being hassled today.

Mrs Green finished writing and turned around. She was wearing her usual white lab coat, buttoned so tight that Malachi wondered how she managed to breathe. When she took it off at night it must leave an angry red line, like a scar, running around her neck.

Mrs Green scanned the tables until her eyes rested on Malachi.

"Glad to see you could join us, Malachi," she said. "But if you daydreamed a little less, perhaps you'd make it to class on time occasionally."

Jarrod sniggered. Malachi looked at the bench. Mrs Green was big on punctuality. In fact, Mrs Green was big on lots of things that Malachi wasn't particularly good at. Like ordering and labelling; putting things in categories; keeping his words and thoughts tidy; neatness.

Today, as she did every day, Mrs Green had written *Order of Lesson* at the top of the whiteboard in black pen. Below this, in blue, she had listed everything they would be covering in class. As they finished each item, Mrs Green liked to give it a big red tick.

Today, under *Order of Lesson*, Mrs Green had written:

Our science projects:

1. *Explain systematic scientific observation*

2. *Describe project parameters*

3. *Outline rules for record taking*

4. *Distribute notebooks.*

Mrs Green rapped her red pen on the desk then pointed at item one.

"In our science projects this term, we will be applying the principles of systematic scientific observation," she said. "Through applying these principles in the context of carefully constructed experiments, then accurately observing and recording the results, science has been able to demystify many previously unexplained phenomena."

Jarrod yawned loudly and rested his head on his hands. Mrs Green ignored him and turned to face the other side of the class. Malachi took the opportunity to shuffle his bag out from between his feet. He lifted out the bottle and balanced it on his knees.

The bottle was certainly heavy. It also smelt: salt and seaweed, mingled with something chemical, like rubber or tar.

Malachi wanted to see inside. He took a swab out of a box on the bench and dipped it in the methylated spirits for the Bunsen burners, then rubbed at the glass until he'd made a clear patch the size of a marble. He bent his head and peered inside.

What he saw made him reel back in surprise.

The bottle slid off his lap. Malachi grappled with both hands, stopping it just before it hit the floor. He tucked it back between his knees.

A hard pellet of damp paper pinged off his cheek.

"What ya got there?" Jarrod hissed.

Malachi turned his knees away and shrugged. "Nothing."

"Don't talk rot," said Jarrod, leaning along

the table and trying to see into Malachi's lap. Malachi pulled his bag up to cover the bottle. "Show me," hissed Jarrod.

"No," said Malachi. "It's private."

Jarrod was the last person in the class he'd show the bottle to. He wasn't exactly a bully, but he was harder than the other kids, with a grown-up swagger and a knowing air. He only shared a bench with Malachi because no one else wanted to sit there. Malachi thought they suited each other – two loners stuck together at the back – but he doubted Jarrod shared his views.

"Show me or I'll stick you with my compass," said Jarrod.

"Jarrod," said Mrs Green. "Leave Malachi alone." She pointed to the second point on her list: *Describe project parameters.* "Now class, as I was saying, we will be working on our projects all term, so it's important to choose a topic that really interests you, something you've always wanted to know more about."

Malachi waited until Jarrod had gone back to sketching skulls on his refill before sliding his bag to one side and peering again through the small window he'd cleared in the glass.

Pointing straight at him was a cannon: a tiny black cannon coated in grime and soot. The cannon was mounted in a wooden wall, and when Malachi turned the bottle slightly, he glimpsed a flap of tatty grey canvas billowing above it. Twisting the bottle down, he made out the frothy top of a grubby grey wave.

"Of course," he whispered. "It's a ship."

Mrs Green rapped her red pen. "Did you have some observation you wanted to share with the class, Malachi?" she asked.

Malachi's head jerked up. "Ah, ah … no," he stammered. "I was just thinking about what you were saying."

"Glad to hear it," said Mrs Green. "But please try not to think out loud."

The class laughed and Malachi slipped the bottle back into his bag.

Mrs Green pointed at item three on her list, *Outline rules for record taking*. Malachi noticed that she'd already placed a tick next to items one and two. He'd missed them.

"You should record everything," Mrs Green said. "Every change in state, appearance and smell. Write it all down in your notebooks as accurately as you can. If you have any questions or reach any conclusions as you go along, write these down too." She placed a red tick beside item three and lowered her pen to hover over item four, *Distribute notebooks*. "We will be using new notebooks for the projects. You may each collect one when class is finished."

As if on cue, the bell rang. Malachi joined the end of the line and filed past to collect his notebook. It was thin, with a blood red cover and pale yellow pages. He had no idea what he was supposed to be writing in it. The science room door banged shut behind him and he glanced back just in time to see Mrs Green, up at the whiteboard, giving her fourth and final point a decisive red tick.

Chapter four

BACK HOME, MALACHI SLUMPED down on the front step. The afternoon stretched emptily before him. Dad would be home later, but he wasn't exactly good company at the moment, and now there wasn't even camping to look forward to: just chores and homework, hanging around the house.

When Mum was alive, weekends had meant adventures. Mum was the type of person who could find an adventure in a supermarket car park. But then she'd died and it was as if Dad had had all the stuffing sucked out of him – the outside of Dad was still there, but the inside, where the spark was, had been vacuumed clean away.

Malachi looked around the garden. What a mess: weeds, weeds and more weeds. He pulled out a few that were growing around the step, just for something to do.

Then he remembered the bottle.

Inside the house, Malachi gathered together all the cleaning things he needed, then carried them to his room and set to work. It was a bit like being at a play, where inch by inch the curtain is being drawn. As the thick salt that encrusted the glass flaked away, more of the ship's hull came into view. Its boards were rough and weather-beaten, thinly covered with black peeling paint. From hatches in the hull, eight cannons, four on either side, poked their blackened muzzles seaward.

More cleaning revealed the ship's deck. It was higher at the prow and stern, surrounded by elaborate curling railings. In the lower middle section, a trapdoor stood open above a shadowy hold. Beside the trapdoor was a pile of green-stained rope, and two open barrels filled with a dark oily liquid.

"Pitch," murmured Malachi. They'd used it in the old days for waterproofing ships' hulls, and it explained the tar he'd smelt in science. Or did it? Surely it wouldn't be real pitch inside the bottle, but something else made to look like pitch, like plasticine or paint? And even if it was real, how had he smelt it through the glass?

Malachi carried on cleaning, scraping away small arcs of salt and slime. Some patches were stubborn, and he scrubbed until his fingers stung.

Three masts rose out of the deck. The central one was thicker and taller than those on either side. Their tops were hidden beneath a large clump of barnacles that covered the bottle's neck and side. But when Malachi looked up into the bottle from its base, he could see a ragged basket at the top of the mast nearest the stern.

"A crow's nest, and that's the mizzenmast," he said, wondering, as he spoke, how he knew the names.

Below the hull, the sea was muddy grey. Choppy waves lapped the ship's prow. Beyond its stern, the blue flukes of a whale's tail rose above the foam.

Malachi kept cleaning. As he worked, he became aware of the sound of the sea. Gentle at first, it gradually grew louder and more insistent, until the suck and splash of the waves filled his head.

Malachi stopped what he was doing and looked out the window. Several low hills separated his house from the beach, and even on the wildest nights, the noise of the sea was never more than a refrigerator's hum on the horizon.

Now the sea sound had stopped.

Malachi shook his head and reached once more for the bottle.

As he did so, a car door slammed. There were footsteps on the porch and Malachi hurriedly slid the bottle under his duvet and the cleaning materials under the bed. He pulled his maths textbook out of his bag and flung himself on the duvet, scrabbling to find the page they'd worked on in class.

His father appeared at his bedroom door. "Homework?" he asked, smiling down at Malachi on the bed.

"Yeah, ahhh … maths," said Malachi.

"Need a hand?"

Malachi's father was a quantity surveyor and adored anything to do with numbers. Distances excited him, as did weights and measurements of any type. Exactitudes, definitudes, quantifications and enumerations. Fractions and flinders and smithereens.

He liked things sharp, accurate and succinct. And he loved maths homework.

Malachi usually welcomed his help, but this evening he just wanted him to go away, so he could get on with his cleaning. "Nah, I'm good thanks," he said.

His father, however, was in no hurry to leave. "How was school today?" he asked.

"Fine."

"You have science?"

"Yep."

"I hope you paid attention?"

"Tried to."

"Glad to hear it."

Malachi sat up. "Dad, I had an idea about camping. I thought we could just go for one night, after work on Friday, that way you'd still have Sunday to …"

His father sighed. "Malachi, we've talked about this."

"But I really want to go away, do something

different. Just for …"

"Look, Malachi, I understand that, but I'm busy, OK? It may not seem like it, but it's an awful lot of work doing all this by myself." His father waved a hand to indicate the house and everything that came with it. "Besides, we can't just drop sticks and take off whenever we feel like it."

"But it's not like we do," said Malachi. "In fact, we never …"

"The answer is no," his father said, stepping away from the door. "It's neither possible nor practical at the moment and that's the end of it. Now I suggest you get on with your homework so it's finished before dinner, and when you have finished, you can come and give me a hand."

Malachi kicked the end of his bed. Mrs Green had said to do their science projects about something that really interested them, but what interesting thing could he study when he was stuck at home, day after day? All the other kids in his class got to go away. Even Jarrod went along in his father's truck sometimes. But not Malachi! Oh no. He had to stay at home and do jobs.

Well this time he wouldn't. Why should he help, when Dad didn't keep his promises? Dad could do the garden on his own.

Malachi rolled onto his stomach and buried his head in his pillow, giving the end of his bed another sharp kick.

Chapter five

MALACHI CARRIED ON CLEANING the bottle after dinner, using a knife to chip off the large barnacles that clung to its side. A second crow's nest came into view, bigger and stronger looking than the first, with a broad red ribbon woven through its brim.

"That's more like it," said Malachi.

The top of the mast came next and, flying from it, a black pennant flag, frozen half-unfurled on the breeze. Malachi attacked another patch of barnacles and the ship's prow appeared, high and angular. A long pole – the bowsprit – extended from it, facing down the bottle's neck. A wooden carving of a lady was suspended below.

Splinters of shell scattered across Malachi's legs as he tried to get a clearer view.

The carved lady was hanging face down above the waves, her paint pitted and scratched, her feet cloaked in algae. A grimy coil of wooden hair, once blonde, but now tinged pale green, wound across her shoulders and down her back like a snake.

"A figurehead," said Malachi, although the term seemed too matter of fact. For, despite her travel scars, the carved lady was beautiful, and although her view down the neck of the bottle was a dead-end one, there was an amused smile upon her lips and a bold glint in her eyes.

When the last of the barnacles were gone, Malachi plunged the bottle in a bucket of soapy water and polished its sides with a soft cloth. When he drew it out again, the glass was clear. Just the faintest blue-green tint remained, as if the bottle had been so long afloat that the sea had stained it.

Inside the bottle, the ship lay at anchor. Its sails were furled, and a web of ropes criss-crossed the masts and decks. As he peered closer, Malachi was surprised to discover he knew the names of the different sails and ropes. There were the topmast shrouds and backstays, the preventer and main stays, all keeping the masts erect. And there were the topgallants and topsails, the spritsails and jibs, fully rigged with halyards and clew lines, ready for release when the ship set sail.

Perhaps his father had read him a book about ships when he was little. It was the sort of thing his father would love; a technical book, with cutaways and grids, where everything was accurately identified and named.

On the deck below the masts, the barrels of pitch looked as if they were steaming, silver threads rising from their open tops like tendrils of cloud. How did you create steam inside a bottle? What would it be made of? Malachi would need his magnifying glass to find out, but it was ages since he'd last seen it.

The magnifying glass had been a birthday present from Mum. For a while he'd taken it everywhere, examining everything he found. A few months before she'd died, they'd visited a beach further down the coast, where large rocks the shape of eggs dropped from the crumbling cliffs. Some of the rocks split as they fell and, if you were lucky, you'd find a fossil trapped inside the stone.

Crouched together on the beach, Mum and Malachi had peered through the magnifying glass at the fossil fragments – delicate traceries of leaves, shells like crescent moons, slender worms as thin as veins.

"You can never look at the world too closely," Mum had said. "The closer you look, the more phenomenal it becomes."

Phenomenal was one of Mum's favourite words. She used it all the time. But in this case, Malachi thought she was right. Encased in the rock, the fossils were like cryptic messages from the ancient universe.

Mum had placed her arm around his shoulders. "You will keep looking at things, won't you Malachi, once I'm gone?"

Malachi had felt the tears starting to rise in his eyes, but he'd nodded and Mum had ruffled his hair. "Good boy. I wouldn't want you to miss anything. And Malachi ..."

"Yes?"

"Remember to look for me too."

"But where will you be?"

"I don't know, love. I haven't been there before. But I know you'll still find me in lots of places, if you look."

Not long after that trip, Mum had got worse and gone into hospital, and Malachi had put the magnifying glass away. He hadn't used it since.

Now he started rummaging through his things looking for it, finding it eventually in his sock drawer. But when he used it to look at the barrels, the steam was gone. The air above them was perfectly clear, with not even a stray wisp curling around the masts.

Malachi lowered the magnifying glass. How strange that the steam had disappeared. It must have been a trick of the light, or a streak of soap left on the glass. Yet he was sure he'd seen it. He felt as if someone had played a prank on him.

Looking through the magnifying glass again, he turned his attention to the rest of the ship. Malachi had seen ships in bottles before at the local museum. Galleons, schooners and sloops, humble junks and jaunty clippers with their make-believe cargoes of oriental spice and tea. But he'd never looked at one quite so closely before, never actually cradled one in his hand.

It was like holding a small world, he thought, a perfect translucent world. Whoever had made this one had gone to extraordinary lengths to make it realistic. Everything on the boat had been painstakingly crafted from the proper materials: wood, sailcloth, rusty iron and rope. Even the rigging that secured the furled sails against the yard arms appeared to have real mildew growing on them.

The sails? Malachi slowly lowered the magnifying glass and stared at the ship. When he'd first seen inside the bottle, surely the sails had been loose? When he'd cleared the small space during science, hadn't he seen tattered grey sails, billowing in the wind?

Malachi closed his eyes and tried to remember. But even though it had only happened that morning he wasn't quite sure. He certainly thought he'd seen sails. But if the sails had been up this morning and were now stowed away, how had that happened?

There was a thud and Malachi jumped. His father was coming down the hall. Malachi crammed the bottle and his unused maths book in his bag.

"All finished?" said his father. Malachi nodded. "I've made cocoa if you want some."

"Great," said Malachi, although his voice sounded high and strained. "I'll come and get it." Reluctantly, he followed his father out of the room.

Chapter six

MALACHI TOOK SEVERAL deep breaths. That had been close, way too close. If his father saw the bottle, he'd make Malachi hand it in to the police. Malachi didn't want to do that. Nor did he want to talk about the bottle with his father. Sometimes it was better to keep things, especially new and interesting things like the bottle, to yourself. That way, no one could butt in on their fabulousness, take away their shine.

In the living room, a wild-haired man was

gesticulating on the TV screen. Lots of other people were milling around in the background, some wearing bright shirts and scarves, others dressed all in green.

"What are you watching?" Malachi asked.

"A documentary about the Waipoua Forest," said his father.

"Waipoua. Where's that?"

"Far north, near Omapere on the Hokianga. It was one of your mother's favourite places."

"Really?" Malachi looked closely at the screen, but there were too many people to see much of the trees. "What are they doing?" he asked.

"Protesting. The council wants to put a new road through, but it would mean cutting down some enormous trees and this lot say it shouldn't happen. They're camped out in the forest, but the council is talking about bringing in the police to evict them."

The wild-haired man was waving his hands

even faster now. One of his hands was loosely clenched, and Malachi wondered if he was going to hit the cameraman. Instead he brought his fist close to the camera and uncurled his fingers. Filling his palm was the largest snail that Malachi had ever seen.

"Wouldn't want that on your cabbages," his father said.

"Pupurangi," the wild-haired man was saying. "Kauri snail. Some of these babies are endangered, but they want to destroy their habitat even more, just for the sake of a road. We need more snails, not cars!"

The camera panned away from the man and around the campsite. There were tents and makeshift shelters strung between trees; fireplaces and tables, and piles of blankets and food. There were a lot of adults talking and laughing, and little kids running around and climbing trees. There were even some young people of about Malachi's age, sitting around what looked like a totem pole, playing drums.

"Looks great," said Malachi. His father snorted into his cocoa. "We could go camping there," said Malachi. "We could join in."

"Yes," said his father. "We could, but we're not. You're going to school and I'm going to work."

Malachi put down his cup and sighed. He hadn't really expected any other answer, but joining the protestors might have been fun. "Thanks for the cocoa," he said.

Back in his room, Malachi looked at the black cross on his calendar. He thought about rubbing it out, but instead took the red notebook out of his school bag. It was supposed to be for writing up his science project, but he had another idea.

He turned to the notebook's first page. *SHIP'S LOG*, he wrote in black pen, going over each letter until the words stood solidly in the middle of the page. Then he stopped. A ship needed a name. He pondered for a while,

twiddling his pen, before writing underneath
SHIP'S LOG, Good Ship Phenomenal.

Turning to the second page he tried to
remember Mrs Green's instructions. First he
wrote the date and time, and then he ruled a
line. The next part was where he was supposed
to record his observations. He began to write
down everything he had noticed about the ship
so far, from the whale's tail at the stern to the
beautiful lady at the prow. He hesitated over the
sails, but eventually wrote: *Sails, mouldy, furled
and secured.* He even wrote down the colour of
the waves: *Mud grey.* When he'd finished he
drew another line underneath.

There wasn't a lot of space left on the page,
but Mrs Green had told them to record any
questions or conclusions they reached as they
went along. Malachi thought for a bit, then
wrote in much smaller letters: *Changes on
board?*

He looked at what he'd written. He'd only

found the ship that morning. It was far too early to be reaching conclusions. Besides, how could what he'd written possibly be right? The ship in a bottle was a model; a very clever model, but a model just the same, and models didn't change. He scribbled the words out.

Chapter seven

MALACHI LAY BACK against the sand dunes, enjoying the warmth beneath his back. He was supposed to be at school, in science to be exact, but he just couldn't face it. Things were tedious enough, without another lecture by Mrs Green about their science projects.

Today they were supposed to be choosing their topics. Most of the other kids would have already chosen. Some would have even started. But when Malachi had mentioned the project to his father that morning, he'd suggested that Malachi might like to dig up one of the nests of ants that were invading their garden, and that he could mow the lawn while he was at it. So Malachi still hadn't thought of a topic, and it was better just to stay away: better to be at the beach.

Malachi loved the beach. He loved the way it had no edges. How the places where an edge might be, like the low tide line or the peaks of the dunes, were actually the start of something else: the land or the sea. He liked to stand at the tide line and stare at the horizon until it blurred, sea bleeding into sky, a crossing place between worlds. He liked, too, the way the waves spread their treasures onto the sand, tempting passers-by – shells and feathers, bits of bone and stone, polished lozenges of glass. Treasures like the ship.

Settling himself further into the sand, Malachi undid his pack and pulled out the bottle. The tiny cannons ranged along the ship's side pointed their muzzles straight at him. Malachi imagined them firing, cannon balls the size of pebbles shattering the glass, leaving the small ship free to set sail.

He scanned the rest of the ship. What he saw made his stomach slide.

The trapdoor to the hold still stood open, with the barrels of pitch alongside, but the grubby rope was gone. In its place was a precarious pile of rough crates, strewing straw from between their slats. What was more, the whale, which yesterday had been swimming at the stern, was now raising its barnacled head near the prow, and on the quarterdeck stood a sailor. A swarthy grubby sailor with a red bandanna tied over one eye and breeches the colour of coal dust. His arms, thick with muscles, were folded across his chest and he was staring out to sea as if at any minute he expected something to appear from beyond the horizon of the bottle's curve.

"He wasn't there before!" Malachi said, clambering to his feet. "He definitely wasn't there before."

Malachi barely noticed the shells that spattered from his feet like sparks, or the small green waves that curled at his toes, as he sprinted towards home. He had only one thing on his mind: the ship!

The wonder of the ship, the amazing secret of it, burnt like a star inside him. It was as if he'd swallowed it whole and now the star fizzed and popped in his stomach, shooting out excitement and light. He wanted to let it out, wanted to tell someone, but the one person who would have believed him wasn't here. He'd have to write it down instead.

Back at home, he got out the ship's log. Turning to a fresh page, he wrote the new date and time at the top, and neatly underlined them.

In the observations section he wrote:

Rope gone.

Crates piled on deck instead.
Whale shifted position.
Sailor.

He had so many questions. How had the ship changed? Who, or what, had changed it? And why? Malachi couldn't even begin to think how to answer. He sucked his pen, then ruled another line. Under it he wrote, *Conclusions*, followed by a single word and a question mark: *Magic?*

But what did that mean? How could it be right? Magic wasn't something you found. Not cast up on the beach. Not in everyday life; certainly not in *his* life. Yet things on board the ship had definitely changed. Any way you looked at it, things were happening in the bottle that hadn't been happening before – phenomenal things. Malachi wasn't about to let them slip by him, just because they were hard to believe.

Carefully he wrote, *Phenomena*, after *Magic*

in his conclusions section. Then he closed the book. That would just have to do for now. Even science, with its impossibly long labels for everything, wouldn't have a name for a ship in a bottle that could change.

Chapter eight

MALACHI COULD TELL by the way his father bellowed his name from the front door that he wasn't happy. "Maaalaaachi!"

"I'm in my room," Malachi called back.

His father stood in the doorway, hands on hips. "Mrs Green phoned me at work today."

"There's a surprise," Malachi muttered.

"She says you weren't in class, that you've been late for science every day this week."

Malachi looked at his hands. There was

nothing to say. His father pressed his palm against his forehead as if he was trying to stick his eyebrows back in place. "I don't see why you've got this issue with science, Malachi. It's only a subject, like all the others."

Malachi grimaced. Clearly his father had never heard Mrs Green in full flight. Metallurgy, micrometry, aetiology, entomology. Literality, veracity, deconstructed, reconstructed. Verisimilitude, exactitude, cognisable, divisible. Science was like being inside a pinball machine, with the bells going and the lights flashing, and doors springing up left, right and centre waiting to knock you off course. And it wasn't just the words; it was the way Mrs Green used them. Like the whole world could be slotted into tidy boxes: measured, categorised, labelled and defined.

Malachi wasn't so sure.

To make things worse, Mrs Green had written, *Has difficulty separating fact from fiction*, in his mid-year report.

"What does she mean by that?" Dad had asked.

Malachi had shrugged, "That I'm a dreamer."

"And are you?"

"No, I just see things differently from her."

Dad hadn't thought that was good enough, so he'd given Mrs Green his phone number, "In case she had any concerns".

Mrs Green had taken the offer to heart. These days, Malachi couldn't sneeze in science without Mrs Green getting on the phone to report it. Obviously, today she'd reported his absence.

"You're grounded, Malachi," his father said. "If you think you're going camping, or anywhere else for that matter, until you start making an effort in science, then you're mistaken."

Great. Just great. It looked like Malachi would be doing his project on the ants in the garden after all. No surprises that Mrs Green was to blame.

Chapter nine

ONCE HIS FATHER had gone, Malachi got out the bottle. It felt heavier than it had that morning, and when he lifted it into the evening sun, he could see why.

Inside, things had changed again. The ship's deck was now piled high with crates, chests and provisions of every kind. On the port side, bushels of hay teetered against the rail, while on the starboard, goats, pigs and hens stared dejectedly from rickety cages.

In the centre of the boat, a second trapdoor had been opened and, not one, but five sailors were busy around it. They seemed a motley crew, clothes patched and faded, skin leathered by the sun. One was missing an arm; another, a leg. Standing to one side was the sailor with the red bandanna. He scowled as he surveyed the laden decks, his jaw set in a grim line.

What were the sailors doing?

The ship looked as if it would sink if they loaded any more on to it. Malachi scanned the waves for the whale, but it had gone. Something else floated on the ship's starboard, though, just below the surface of the sea. Malachi twisted the bottle, but he couldn't make out what it was. Instead, with each twist, the water turned a kaleidoscope of the object's colours – pink, green, shimmering gold. It was impossible for Malachi to fix on the object's shape in amongst them.

Malachi gave up and reached for the ship's

log, starting to list the latest changes.

Animals on board. Goats for milk, chickens for eggs, pigs for fresh meat.

New barrels. Fresh water?

Crew of six loading …

Malachi lowered his pen. Now he knew what the sailors were doing; they were preparing for a journey. Why else would they fill the hold with cargo? Why else bring enough provisions on board to last a month?

Skipping to the conclusions section, Malachi wrote, *Preparations for journey underway. Destination …*

Where did the crew think they were going? The ship was trapped in a thick glass bottle with a bung in the neck. There was nowhere to head that wasn't a dead end. Yet the tiny sailors were hard at work, as if, bottle or no bottle, hell or high water, they were going to make a journey.

Malachi added a large black question mark

after *Destination …?* But even as he added it, he realised he had an answer – his answer, if not the ship's.

If the ship, trapped inside a bottle, could go on a journey, then so could he. An adventure, a trip, a quest: it was exactly what he needed. Not possible, not practical, his father had said, yet neither was it possible for a ship in a bottle to change, and this one definitely did.

Malachi began to hop around the room in excitement. Dad could stay home and mope all he liked; he, Malachi, was going to have some fun. But where would he go? The sailors looked like they knew where they were going; what about him?

The answer came easy: Waipoua Forest. He could join the protestors, camp out, watch stars, play drums, help save the trees. He might even be able to get his hands on a snail. Malachi grinned. Imagine Mrs Green's face when he turned up in class with a gigantic snail. It would be the perfect science project.

He sat down at his desk. He needed to get organised. He must, in Mrs Green's words, be systematic. What would he need? What should he take? Grabbing the ship's log, he turned to the back page and wrote *Malachi's Journey* across the top in big letters. Then he started to make a list.

Chapter ten

BY THE TIME HIS FATHER called him for
dinner, Malachi had twenty-five items listed
in the ship's log. It seemed a lot to find and do,
but he must be properly prepared. This could
be the biggest journey of his life. He needed to
get it right.

Making the list was the easy part. It was late
and the house quiet by the time Malachi added
the last item to the pile in his room. The main
problem was that most of the stuff he needed

was in the kitchen or the hall cupboard, and he had to keep walking past his father, who was watching TV in the living room, in order to get it.

At one point his father had stopped him. "What have you got there?" he'd asked.

Malachi looked at the map of the North Island clutched in his hands. "It's a map. It's for my, ahh … science project."

"Your project is on maps?"

"Ahhh … no. Habitats. Snail habitats."

His father laughed. "You liked my garden idea then."

"Yeah, sort of."

Malachi shifted uncomfortably. He didn't like lying to his father, but he could hardly tell him what he was planning. Then he remembered the tough little sailors in the bottle, all working hard to get ready for their journey. They wouldn't let a little bit of discomfort put them off.

"Actually, it's a group project," he said. "We're going to study the snails in all of our gardens and, umm, you know, compare them. So I might be away one night, maybe a couple, because that's when the snails come out, at night, so I'll need to stay over."

His father looked at him closely. "But you're grounded."

Malachi stared back at him. "But this is for my science project. You told me to make an effort and that's what I'm trying to do."

"Hmm. Who else is in your group?"

"Ahh … Jarrod."

"His father drives a truck, doesn't he? You haven't stayed with him before?"

Malachi shook his head. He never went around to his classmates' houses, let alone stay the night, but Dad didn't notice stuff like that.

"Well, make sure it's a weekend," his father said. "And get his father to ring me." He levered himself out of his chair. "That map you've got isn't going to be much use. You'll need a local one, if you're studying local habitats." His father took the map from Malachi's hand and disappeared into the hall with it, returning with one of their town. "This'll be much better," he said.

Things got easier once his father went to bed. Malachi found the old backpack his mother had used for tramping, and managed to swap back the local map for the one he really wanted: the one showing the Waipoua Forest. Eventually, he'd collected everything he needed. Now all he had to do was jam it into the backpack.

Suddenly Malachi was bone tired. He kicked off his jeans and collapsed onto his bed. Packing would have to wait.

The bottle made an uncomfortable lump under his pillow, but Malachi couldn't be bothered moving it. It would be dark inside the bottle now, night-time on board the ship. Malachi imagined the tiny sailors rolling and snoring in their bunks, catching up on sleep before their big journey. He wondered if, like him, they had finished loading their cargo. If in the morning they could weigh anchor and set sail.

The thought made him sit up again.

Snatching the ship's log off the floor, he consulted his list one more time. He'd put a big red tick beside twenty-four of the twenty-five items, but there was still one thing left to be done. He'd been so busy collecting stuff, that he'd overlooked the most important item: *Transport.*

Without Dad, how could he get to the forest? The sailors had their boat, but he only had a bike, and he could hardly cycle to the top of the North Island. He had some money, but not a lot. Certainly not enough for a long-distance bus ticket.

Malachi threw the ship's log across the room. It hit the wall and fluttered to the floor like a stunned bird. His father was right – he wasn't going anywhere. Like the ship, Malachi was stuck exactly where he was.

Chapter eleven

MALACHI WISHED THE BELL would go. The disappointment of his scuppered plans had hung over him all day. All he wanted to do was go home and go to bed.

Up at the whiteboard, Mrs Green was droning on again about how amazing science was. She pointed her pen at the next point on her list, *Follow up on projects.*

"Malachi, I don't believe we've heard from you yet about your science project. Perhaps you'd like to share with the class what it's about?"

Malachi sighed. He may as well get it over with. "Snails," he said. "Snails and their habitats. I have a map and I'm going to mark on it where I find them."

"Very good," said Mrs Green.

"Then I'm going to take them on an adventure," said Malachi.

Some of the class started laughing.

"An adventure?" said Mrs Green.

"Yeah," said Malachi. "Like a road trip, but in a big bottle. Snails don't usually do stuff like that, so I'll be able to study how they adapt."

More of the class started laughing. Even Jarrod stopped carving *Death* into his desk with his compass and looked at Malachi. Mrs Green looked stunned.

"I see," she said. "Have you recorded your plans in your notebook, Malachi?"

"Not really."

Malachi reached for the ship's log, but he was too late. Jarrod's hand shot down the table and snatched the notebook from under Malachi's pencil case.

"Give it back," said Malachi, trying to grab the notebook, but Jarrod had started rifling through the pages.

"He's written quite a bit," he said. "He's written …"

"Jarrod, please give the journal back to Malachi immediately," said Mrs Green.

"But you'll never guess what he's written." Jarrod started spluttering. "As one of his conclusions, he's written that it's magic, magic ph-ph-ph …"

The whole class was laughing now. Mrs Green loosened the collar of her lab coat.

"Magic, Malachi?" she said.

"It was a question," said Malachi, snatching the notebook back out of Jarrod's hand. "It wasn't a conclusion."

"Magic is not something that generally comes into science," said Mrs Green. "Perhaps you and I had better have a chat about your project later?"

Malachi scowled. He examined the ship's log. Its cover had twisted in the tussle with Jarrod, but otherwise it was OK. He should never have brought it to school today.

He caught Jarrod's eye. "What d'you do that for?" he hissed.

Jarrod smirked. "Stupid thing to write. You should take a leaf out of my book." He held his notebook by the corner, so the pages fanned open. It was completely blank.

"At least I wrote something," said Malachi. "What's she going to say about that?"

"Don't give a toss," said Jarrod. "Come Saturday, I'm on the road with my old man."

"Lucky you," said Malachi. He wished he could say the same.

"Big run this time," said Jarrod. "All the

way up to Omapere, and there ain't gonna be a science teacher or test tube in sight. By the time I get back, it'll be too late to start anything. What a shame!" Jarrod jiggled his empty notebook in the air, and despite himself, Malachi smiled.

Chapter twelve

WHEN CLASS ENDED, Malachi slunk out the door before Mrs Green noticed him. He wandered home along the beach, but today there was no pleasure to be found there.

The fine sand along the dunes lifted on the breeze, small pebbles knocked and rolled on the tide line, and the waves swayed in and out in their never-ending dance. Everything was on the move, everything shifting and changing. It was only Malachi who was stuck in one place.

At home, Malachi pulled the ship in a bottle out from under his bed. There had been developments on board. Most of the cargo had been stowed away and, apart from the animals in their cages, the decks were clear. There was a quality of stillness about the ship, a readiness in its tidy rigging and swept decks. Even the sea was poised, its usual chop smoothed to a blanket of grey, while up above, dank mist crowded the topmasts, muffling the ship and all that lay below.

Yet in the shadows, something glinted: a flash of silver, an emerald gleam, lightening the ship's starboard. It was the object Malachi had spotted yesterday, but now, with the still sea and strange light, he could make out what it was.

A mermaid! Swimming alongside the ship's hull, her scaled tail curved like a question mark across the surface of the sea. She swam head down, her long hair fanning out behind her, cloaking her shoulders.

Malachi looked for other changes, but after a couple of minutes put the bottle on his pillow and stretched out on his back. There was something about the afternoon's science lesson that bothered him; something other than the magic episode. He replayed what had happened: Mrs Green's questions, his answers, Jarrod snatching the notebook, the class laughing. But that wasn't what niggled him. It was something else, something later.

Malachi rolled on to his stomach and peered into the bottle. The mermaid hadn't moved, and he was unable to see her face. He saw someone else though.

Hunkered deep within a stack of barrels on the starboard side was a boy. He had bare feet, a tattered shirt and red-striped shorts, and was crouched so low among the shadows that, were it not for his mop of sandy hair, he might have been part of them.

The boy was hiding, although none of the sailors seemed to be looking for him or even aware that he was there. They were all too busy going about their business or gazing thoughtfully at the glass horizon.

He must be a stowaway, thought Malachi, and the thought was like a key turning in his mind.

"A stowaway," he said, as with sudden clarity he understood what it was about the afternoon's science lesson that had been bugging him.

Malachi started digging around in the abandoned pile of provisions for his journey. He found the map and flipped it open, running a trembling finger over the network of towns and settlements that threaded the shores of the Hokianga Harbour.

"Rawene, Whirinaki, Pakanae, Opononi … Omapere."

Omapere! That was it! The place where Jarrod's father was heading in his truck. And it was just as Malachi hoped, because there, less than a centimetre away along State Highway 12, was the Waipoua Forest. What's more, tomorrow was Saturday. The Jarrods would be leaving and he would be with them, stowed away in the back of their truck. His journey was about to begin.

Chapter thirteen

COOL BLUE SHADOWS, like stains left by the night, filled the truck yard. The high wire fence surrounding it twinkled with wobbling dew. It was just after dawn and no truckies had arrived yet. Malachi had the yard to himself.

He was hungry, but he tried to ignore it. The backpack was smaller than he'd thought and he'd had to leave behind a lot of the food, as well as the spare bottle of water and the blanket. Then, at the last minute, it looked like he was going to have to leave the ship in a bottle behind too.

Malachi had always assumed that the ship would be making the trip north with him. But even when he'd packed and repacked everything, there was still no room for it. He'd considered leaving it in his bedside drawer; after all, what practical use would it be? Then he'd noticed that the mermaid had moved.

She was swimming in front of the ship now, her hair spread around her like a silver net. She had turned over onto her back, and although her face remained below the waves, he could see clearly that she was smiling. She also had one arm extended above her head, as if pointing in the direction that the ship would soon be heading. Malachi desperately wanted to know where that might be.

So he'd taken out his woolly socks and raincoat and added them to the pile of discarded items. With a hefty shove, he'd flattened just enough space for the bottle and ship's log, then quickly refastened the pack's top before the whole lot sprang out again.

Now the pack was beginning to feel heavy, and Malachi decided to look for Jarrod's father's truck. It didn't take long. In the yard's far corner was a small, shabby, red truck with *Dobbs and Son, General Rural Carriers* written on its side in curvy cream letters. Dobbs was Jarrod's last name. He must be the 'Son'.

Malachi walked quickly around the truck testing the doors. They were all locked, so he found a space behind a nearby shed where he could wait without being seen. To take his mind off his stomach, he got out the ship's log and read back through his list, grinning when he got to *Transport*. Using his red pen he gave it an enormous tick. Then he turned back to his last log entry and carefully wrote an answer next to his unanswered question: *Destination? Waipoua.* His grin grew even broader.

He put the ship's log back in his bag. He was too excited to write any more, although his excitement was edged with discomfort. He didn't like deceiving his father. But what could he do? Dad refused to get on with his life. Did that mean Malachi had to sit around too? Besides, this journey was something he had to do: the ship was telling him so.

Malachi's thoughts were interrupted by the sound of an engine, as a ute swung into the truck yard, braking hard at the last moment and sending up a spray of gravel. There were loud voices from inside the cab, before a man climbed out clutching a clipboard.

"Get on with it boy, you'll make us late," he said.

Malachi would have recognised Jarrod's father, Mr Dobbs, anywhere. He had the same swagger and the same thickset shoulders, his head bobbing about on top of them, as if he'd lost his neck. Jarrod himself emerged from the cab, lugging two enormous sports bags. He dragged them over to the truck while his father consulted his clipboard.

"All over the friggin' place," Mr Dobbs said. "Ohura, Te Kuiti, Te Kauwhata, Pukekohe, Ramarama, then, let's see, nothing until Omaha, but then there's Waipu …"

The list continued. Most of the places Malachi had never heard of, although some he recognised as being up north. He'd hoped for a direct trip. Clearly that wasn't on the cards.

Jarrod went past carrying two large flagons, which he filled from a tap. He left them at the back of the truck, then cleaned the windscreen, propped open the bonnet, cleared a collection of old cups and food wrappers from out of the truck's cab, unlocked the large double doors on the trailer, loaded the flagons and came to stand beside his father, who was still muttering over his clipboard.

"What do you want?" Mr Dobbs asked.

Jarrod scuffed the gravel with his toe. "You know that big job you talked about? You're not going to do it, are you Dad? You're not going to go through with it?"

Mr Dobbs lowered his clipboard and scowled at him. "Why else do you think I was talkin' about it?"

"But Dad ..." said Jarrod.

"Before you bleedin' ask, for the bleedin' money, that's why. Some of those animals are worth a fortune."

"But they're protected, Dad. We learnt about them at school. It's against the law."

"Why do you think they're worth so much? Don't be stupid, Jarrod. If you're going to be stupid, you can darn well stay at home."

"But what if you get caught?" said Jarrod. "What would happen to me?"

"We're not gonna get caught, all right? Not if you keep your mouth shut and do as you're told. I've discussed it with Flint and it's all set to go, once we get up north. Now stop being an idiot, and check the oil and water. There's just what's-her-name's delivery we're waiting on. I'm gonna make a cup of tea."

Mr Dobbs sauntered off towards a hut on the far side of the yard. Malachi inched forward until he could see into the back of the truck's trailer. Something large was stacked down its far end, against the wall behind the cab, but otherwise it was empty. Jarrod was busy at the front of the truck. Malachi slipped out from behind the shed.

It was less than ten metres to the back of the truck, but it seemed like an endless expanse. Malachi was painfully aware of every footfall, every knocked stone. He made it without alerting Jarrod, though, and was just reaching out for the back ledge, when a small green car towing a clattering trailer rounded the corner into the yard and stopped in front of the truck.

Malachi sprinted back behind the shed.

He would have recognised that car anywhere, even without its personalised number plate.

"Dad, the load's arrived," Jarrod called, as Mrs Green pushed open her car door and stepped briskly out into the yard.

Chapter fourteen

Mrs Green's car was lime green, with a kinky bonnet and narrow wheels. Mrs Green was very proud of it. She said it was French. Malachi thought it looked like a baked bean can that had been run over by a lawnmower. He also thought the *Greeny* number plate was juvenile, and not at all what you would expect from the grumpiest teacher in school. He was amazed it was powerful enough to tow a trailer, let alone a trailer carrying a very large object swathed in bubble wrap.

The large object was obviously heavy. Jarrod and his father struggled to unload it, as Mrs Green stood to one side and barked directions. She was wearing a pair of jeans, trainers and a crimson puffer jacket, but still looked exactly as if she was giving a science lesson.

"Careful, careful, it's very sensitive," she kept saying. "Be careful not to knock it."

Mr Dobbs' face had gone an alarming shade of red, and the sleeves of his chequered shirt bulged as he manoeuvred the object first onto a trolley and from there into the truck's trailer. Jarrod clambered in after it and secured it to the wall with thick straps, while his father stood with Mrs Green in the middle of the yard and consulted his clipboard.

"Make us that cup of tea will you Jarrod?" he said.

Jarrod trotted dutifully off to the hut. Malachi eased back out from behind the shed.

"So you're thinking it will be early Sunday afternoon?" said Mrs Green.

"Sounds about right," said Mr Dobbs.

"Any later and I'd be pushing to get back."

Mrs Green bent down to pick up her bag. Malachi froze. He was halfway between the shed and the truck. If Mrs Green glanced behind her now, his game would be up. "Of course, they're no longer there," she said, straightening up.

Mr Dobbs grunted. "Give it up did they?"

"In a way," said Mrs Green. "They left a couple of days ago."

Jarrod came out of the hut with his father's tea. Malachi jumped as if he'd been stuck with a cattle prod. If he didn't get in the trailer immediately, his journey was going to end right here, right now, before it even started. With a leap an athlete would be proud of, he vaulted up and onto the tailgate, and scuttled towards the shadows at the trailer's far end.

Chapter fifteen

THE LARGE OBJECT at the back of the trailer turned out to be a sofa. Luckily for Malachi, it had been loaded with its back facing the door, so its seat formed a shadowy alcove where he could lie without being seen. A label pinned on one of its cushions read: *Mrs H. MacKintyre, 15A Main Road, Omapere.*

Perfect, thought Malachi, as he settled himself down. Not only was he going to be delivered where he wanted to go, but he would travel there in comfort. The trailer smelled strongly of fusty blankets and stale vegetables. The only other delivery item in it so far was Mrs Green's bubble-wrapped object. Malachi could still hear her, talking to Mr Dobbs. Then her car started and he heard her drive away.

After that, a long time passed with no sound at all. Malachi was beginning to wonder if the trip had been cancelled, when he heard hurried footsteps and the trailer doors closed. The cab doors slammed, and the engine rumbled into life.

Malachi sat up. "We're on the road," he said.

With the doors closed, it was black as gunpowder in the back of the trailer. Malachi fumbled around in his backpack until he found his torch. He flicked it to low beam, undid the top of the pack and pulled out the bottle.

Although its position in the bottle was unchanged, the ship was now underway. Its rigging was taut, its flags streamed and its mainsails billowed in an unfelt wind. The mermaid was there, swimming alongside. She'd flipped her tail down and raised her head and shoulders out of the waves, so Malachi could see her face clearly for the first time. Her eyes were as bright and clear as the sea on a sunny day, and she was still smiling – straight at him.

Malachi wasn't sure what to do. Of all the people he'd spotted so far in the bottle, none of them had noticed him. It was as if their gazes, like the ship, were enclosed in the bottle, unable to reach beyond the glass horizon that formed the edge of their world. But the mermaid was looking outwards, or so it seemed to Malachi, through the coarse glass and straight into his eyes.

The truck swung around a corner and Malachi steadied the torch against his chest. Holding the bottle in front of the beam, he scanned the rest of the ship.

There were eight or nine sailors on deck now,

all clustered down one end. In their midst was the boy that Malachi had spotted earlier. He'd been hauled out of his hiding place and a sailor in a dirty jerkin had him by the ear, while the one with the red bandanna poked him with a stick. The sailors did not look pleased with their find. In fact, they looked livid. The boy, however, appeared defiant, as if he knew that, now they were at sea, there was not a lot the sailors could do. Malachi doubted he would be so brave if the Jarrods discovered him.

He turned the bottle around and something else caught his eye. From the mainmast, another flag had been hoisted. It was large and black, with a bold white pattern in its middle. The mist that had shrouded the ship earlier still curled around it, making it difficult to see.

Malachi flicked the torch beam to full and angled it into the top of the bottle. He gulped. Grinning from the flag's dark centre was an evil eyeless skull, laid across a gleaming pair of crossed bones. It was the Jolly Roger – the trademark of pirates and favoured flag of cut-throats and lawless seafarers everywhere.

The truck swung around another corner, hit a bump and hung suspended for a spilt second above the road, before crashing down and sending the torch flying from Malachi's hands. There was the tinkle of fine glass breaking and the beam went out, plunging Malachi back into darkness, the bottle clutched between his suddenly sweaty palms.

Chapter sixteen

AFTER HE GOT OVER the shock, Malachi decided he was pleased that the ship belonged to pirates. It was better, after all, than sharing his journey with something mundane, like a cargo ship, or depressing, like a ship full of slaves.

Pirates at least were adventurous, and adventure was what this trip was all about. It was just a shame that, with the truck's doors closed and his torch gone, it was too dark to keep watch on events inside the bottle.

It was also too dark to write in the ship's log, and too bumpy besides, as despite the sofa, Malachi was jolted and jounced every time the truck hit an uneven patch of road. As soon as he could though, he'd have to change the ship's name in the log. You couldn't have a pirate ship named *Good.* It would have to be the *Bad Ship Phenomenal* from now on.

Instead, Malachi lay back and thought about the journey ahead. Even with all the stops, they should be at Omapere by late afternoon. From there, it couldn't be more than twenty kilometres back to the Waipoua Forest. He could hitch that. If there was a phone, he'd ring his father once he got there, just to let him know he was safe. Dad was bound to be annoyed, but he had no one but himself to blame. Besides, Malachi only planned to stay a couple of days. Then he'd head home.

It was warm in the back of the truck and, despite the bumpy ride, Malachi began to doze off. He was just drifting towards the comforting no-man's land between awake and asleep, when the truck started to slow down, then stopped. He checked his watch. They'd been travelling for less than an hour.

The trailer's doors swung open. Mr Dobbs was standing by the tailgate with another man, who was wearing a wide-brimmed black hat that concealed most of his face. Behind them was a forklift, with a large cage balanced high up on its raised prongs. There was a strong smell of silage.

"Two hits this time," said the man in the black hat.

"Two?" said Mr Dobbs. "I thought there was just the big one. Up north."

"I took the liberty of arranging another," said the man. "Increasing our takings you might say. It's in Helensville. An overnighter. The rig you're after is Watson's. You know it? He never locks it."

Mr Dobbs nodded. "What is it?"

"Royal jelly."

"Royal bleedin' jelly!"

"Liquid gold that stuff. People pay good money for it."

Mr Dobbs looked sceptical, but he made a note on his clipboard.

"The second one's the big haul from Blacko up north," said the man. "But you already know about that. He'll phone you when he's made the drop, but make sure you wait half an hour before pick up. Apparently there's been a whole lotta do-gooders sniffing around." The man stopped talking as Jarrod appeared at the end of the truck. "What's the boy doing here?"

"He's coming with me," said Mr Dobbs.

"Bit risky ain't it?" said the man.

"That's up to me, isn't it? You organise the gigs, and I pull them off. That's the arrangement. Anyway, Jarrod here'll be a good decoy, if I need one."

"As long as he doesn't give the game away," the man said.

"More than his life's worth," said Mr Dobbs. "Jarrod, this is Flint, Mr Flint to you. You might say he was my business partner."

Jarrod nodded glumly.

Flint pointed to the large cage balanced on the prongs of the forklift. "And I got you an extra delivery. It's a runt for ma sister. She's at Mamaranui. It's on your way."

"Only just." Mr Dobbs glowered at the cage. "Looks pretty sickly. You sure it'll make it?"

"Doesn't matter if it doesn't. She's only gonna slaughter it come Christmas."

Mr Dobbs consulted his clipboard. "Tell her tomorrow afternoon."

Tomorrow afternoon! Malachi's heart sank. He'd only brought enough food and water for one day, and then not a lot.

"A day here or there won't matter," said Flint, climbing into the forklift.

The animal in the cage let out a high-pitched squeal as Flint lowered the cage into the back of the truck.

"Coming in for a cuppa?" he called, as he backed the forklift away.

"Right you are," said Mr Dobbs. "Get a move on, Jarrod."

Malachi waited until their footsteps had died away, then raised his head cautiously over the top of the sofa. The cage was only a couple of metres away, and in it, with its backside turned to him, was a small, very dirty piglet. Malachi slipped over the sofa's back. The piglet's ears twitched, but it carried on snuffling in its food tray. Malachi sidled up to the cage.

"Hello piggy," he whispered.

All four of the piglet's feet left the ground at once. One moment it had its back to Malachi, the next its snout was centimetres from his face. Malachi found himself looking straight into a pair of small dark eyes, set in a surprisingly clean face. The face was pink, except for a dark triangular patch around one eye.

"I was just going to say," whispered Malachi, "that it might pay to pace yourself. It looks like we might be in for a long trip."

The piglet's snout curled slowly upwards, and it emitted a squeal that would curdle milk. There was the sound of running feet, and Malachi leapt back over the sofa as Jarrod lunged onto the tailgate of the truck.

At the sight of Jarrod, the piglet backed into the far corner of its cage and started squealing fit to bust. Flint appeared, pushed Jarrod out of the way and gave the cage a vicious kick. The piglet stopped squealing and fixed Flint with a wild-eyed stare.

"For cripes' sake, Jarrod," yelled Mr Dobbs, who had followed close behind Flint. "What are you doing up there?"

"J … just checking out the pig," said Jarrod.

"This isn't a bleedin' school trip to the zoo,"

Mr Dobbs yelled. "Now close up, we're going."

Jarrod climbed down. He turned and stared into the trailer for a moment, before closing the doors. Seconds later the truck's engine started up. The piglet began to squeal, but thought better of it and, as they set off, Malachi could hear it scuffling in the straw on the bottom of its cage, the sound punctuated by the occasional self-pitying squeak.

Chapter seventeen

BY LUNCHTIME THEY'D PICKED up a loom, a chafe separator, three large drums full of stinky sloshing liquid, and two sealed hives of bees whose angry buzzing joined the piglet's squeals every time the truck took a corner too fast.

Malachi was beginning to wish he'd found out what exactly Mr Dobbs carried before he'd embarked on this trip. He'd eaten half his sandwiches and an orange, but he was still hungry. Worse than that was his growing need to pee. He thought about relieving himself in the corner, but when he remembered all the hours he still had to spend in the trailer, he couldn't bring himself to do it. He would just have to find a way to get out without being seen.

In theory, there were plenty of opportunities. A piano, a weed-eater, four bales of wool, a worm farm and a rusty car bonnet joined the rest of the load, until Malachi wondered how they would fit more in tomorrow. At every stop, he inched his way forward, but either Jarrod or his father would always be standing just beyond the trailer's back doors, making escape impossible.

By the time they got to the truck depot at Cambridge, Malachi's bladder felt full to the point of popping. Jarrod and his father lounged against the tailgate, looking like they were in no hurry to go anywhere. Malachi decided to distract himself by checking on the ship.

There were pirates everywhere: on the decks, around the trapdoors, in the rigging. Malachi wondered where they'd been hiding until now. He also wondered what they'd been doing, as none of them looked happy – their faces were grim, their stance determined.

At the bow, the pirate with the red bandanna had a telescope clasped to his good eye. The telescope was trained beyond the figurehead, into the neck of the bottle. From the crow's nests, two other pirates pointed the same way.

Two further sets of cannons had appeared in the ship's stern, while on the quarterdeck, masses of armaments lay ranged in tidy piles. Cutlasses, daggers, gleaming flintlock pistols, with dusty powder horns stacked alongside. Glinting kopi, their curved blades like wicked smiles; rope-bound axes, long-barrelled muskets, chain-shot and grappling irons, all tidily sorted and stacked.

Sailing the high seas must be a dangerous business, thought Malachi. Then he saw what the pirates were pointing at. Protruding into the neck of the bottle, from somewhere beyond the bung, was a bowsprit. Another bowsprit meant another ship, and it was headed into the bottle.

Malachi was amazed, although he suspected he shouldn't be. If his ship could change, then why shouldn't another appear? Still, he couldn't quite believe it. For a start, where was the new ship coming from? So far, only its prow had made it into the bottle, so where was the rest of it? And what business did it have with the pirates?

If Malachi didn't quite believe it, the pirates did. There was urgency in their gestures and menace in their eyes. Even the stowaway had been put to work, and was crouched beside a barrel, measuring scoops of gunpowder into twists of paper.

"A fight," Malachi whispered. "There's going to be a fight." Either that or a raid, and the pirates were preparing to plunder the newcomers' ship.

Mr Dobbs dropped his clipboard on the tailgate and Malachi jumped: he'd forgotten the Jarrods were there.

"There's Bill Kidd," said Mr Dobbs. "I'm off to have a word."

"He's not in on it, is he?" said Jarrod. "The big job?"

"Will you stop going on about it," said Mr Dobbs. "And no, he's not. It's just you, me, Blacko and Flint, so don't go opening your big trap to anyone else. Now I'm off to talk business. You stay here and keep an eye on that damned pig. I don't trust it."

"But I need to go to the loo," said Jarrod.

"Well go then. Just make sure you don't talk to anyone."

Mr Dobbs ambled in the direction of the blue truck. Jarrod scuttled in the direction of the toilets.

Malachi decided to seek some relief of his own. He pushed through the jumble of objects in the back of the truck until he was standing on the corner of the tailgate. He watched with satisfaction as his pee made a dusty puddle on the hard ground, then retreated to the sofa with a contented sigh.

After a few minutes, Jarrod came back and sat on the tailgate. He threw a small silver object from hand to hand.

"Look," he said, when his father returned. "I found it in the toilet. It's a bullet."

Mr Dobbs snorted. "That's not a bullet, you idiot." He grabbed the object and pulled it in two. "It's a flaming lipstick."

"Oh." Jarrod looked crestfallen. Then his face brightened. "I could keep it for Mum. She likes pink."

Mr Dobbs turned an alarming shade of pink himself. He raised his arm and threw the two halves of the lipstick over the fence.

"Don't ever mention your mother to me," he snarled.

Jarrod flinched. Behind him, the piglet began to squeak softly.

Mr Dobbs turned to leave, then stopped and raised his boot.

"Jarrod, ya filthy little blighter," he roared. "You could have used the bleedin' toilet."

"But I did," said Jarrod. "That's where I got the …"

"Don't lie to me," roared his father. "I've just stepped in your bleedin' pee. You can clean my bleedin' boots before you go to bleedin' bed. Now shut up this damned truck before I leave you and that rodent animal here in Cambridge."

Jarrod's face quivered as he shut the doors.

"Sorry," whispered Malachi.

Soon after, the truck set off again. This time, they followed a long stretch of road, mercifully without stops. When they finally turned off, night was on its way.

The new road was windy. Malachi braced himself against the back of the sofa, but with every swerve he was rolled from one side of the seat to the other. By the time the truck eventually stopped, he was beginning to retch.

He curled up in a sad ball on the sofa. It was dark now and was growing cold. He was alone, with very little food, hardly any water, no blanket, and no idea where, or how far away from his destination, he was. Worst of all, even though the truck had stopped, he truly, honestly felt like he was going to be sick.

And then he was. Straight down the back of Mrs MacKintyre's sofa.

Chapter eighteen

THE NIGHT WAS PITCH BLACK when Malachi woke up. Something, or rather someone, was moving around outside the truck.

"Dad," came an urgent whisper. "Dad, I ..."

"Shurrup," was the muffled reply.

"But I want to go back to bed."

"I said shurrup," said the other voice, as the doors of the truck began to open.

Outside the truck were two dark figures. The big one was holding a lantern. The light moved, and Malachi saw Mr Dobbs. He looked even bigger than usual in a bulky black coat, a black beanie and a scarf wrapped commando-style across his face. Jarrod stood to the side, with his hands tucked into his armpits. He was wearing his pyjamas.

"You stay here," said Mr Dobbs. "If anyone comes, head 'em off."

"How?"

"Distract them. Pretend you're sleepwalking or something. Give me time to get away."

Jarrod moved into the circle of light.

"Can I keep the lantern?" he asked.

"Course you bleedin' can't," said Mr Dobbs. "I'll need it to find the stuff."

"But I don't want to stay out here by myself in the dark." Jarrod's voice began to rise. Mr Dobbs clapped his hand across Jarrod's mouth.

"You trying to get us caught? Watson's rig's just over there. I'll be in and out. If you see anyone, anyone at all, make sure you get to them before they get to me. It'll be good practice for tomorrow." Mr Dobbs dropped his hand and shoved Jarrod towards the truck. "And Jarrod?"

"What?"

"Don't get too scared of the darky warky, will you?"

Jarrod hunched on the corner of the tailgate, his knees pulled to his chin. He sniffled into them.

Malachi felt sorry for him. His own father may be a bit of a bore, but at least he didn't drag him out in his pyjamas in the middle of the night and call him names. If this was a life of adventure on the road, Malachi was no longer sure he wanted it.

After what seemed like an age, Mr Dobbs came back, his breath rasping behind his scarf.

"Here's the loot," he said, sliding three wooden crates into the truck. Jarrod eyed them suspiciously.

After two more trips, there were ten crates piled next to Jarrod. Their pale wood glowed in the lamplight.

"Man's asking for it if he can't even lock his bleedin' truck," Mr Dobbs said.

Jarrod muttered into his knees. "It's still stealing."

"Oooo. Getting all high and mighty on us now are you? I'll have you know, young Jarrod, that this stealing is what's going to put food in your mouth for the next month. Anyway it's not stealing, it's relieving."

"Same thing," said Jarrod.

"No it's not. Relieving is freeing people who have too much stuff from what they don't need. Just like, what's his name, the guy who lived in the forest."

"Tarzan?"

"No, not bleedin' Tarzan. Robin Hood. We're just like him."

"Robin Hood didn't keep the stuff, Dad,"

Jarrod said. "He took from the rich and gave to the poor."

"Well you can forget that, we're keeping our cut. We're like highwaymen, then, like the Lone Ranger."

Jarrod pouted. "The Lone Ranger wasn't a highwayman, and he didn't steal."

"OK then, Captain Hook."

"But Captain Hook's a pirate," said Jarrod.

"So that's what we are, isn't it?" said Mr Dobbs. "Highway pirates, sneaking on board other people's ships and taking their stuff, then sailing away on the high seas."

"But we're in a truck," said Jarrod.

"Truck, ship, what's the difference? It's the daring that counts, the swashbuckling attitude."

Mr Dobbs started swaggering up and down, making mock sword thrusts at Jarrod and the crates. "Royal bleedin' jelly, aye? Doubt the poor would even want the stuff. Tomorrow will be a different story. That loot will be worth something."

Jarrod started sniffling again and his father pushed him off the tailgate. "Stop blubbing and give me a hand to lock up. I'm off back to bed."

Chapter nineteen

AFTER THEY'D GONE, Malachi tried to settle to sleep on the sofa, but it was no good. The cushions were full of lumps and humps, and every time he moved, the night air slid another frozen finger under his clothes.

His thoughts bothered him too. Jarrod needed help, and Malachi was the only one here to help him. But what could he do? It was hard to come up with a plan when his own situation seemed far from promising.

By the time a gradual lightening in the air announced that dawn was on its way, Malachi was hungry, thirsty and cold. Outside the trailer, an early bird croaked its waking notes, but other than that the only sounds were piglet's gentle snores and the increasingly demanding rumbles from Malachi's stomach.

He ate his remaining food and allowed himself a tiny sip of water, then levered himself stiffly off the couch. It was definitely dawn now. Bright thin lines of light sliced into the trailer through ventilation slits set high up on its walls. Malachi pulled the ship in a bottle out of his bag and, holding it carefully, climbed on to the lid of the piano and lifted it into the light.

A sea fog had risen in the bottle overnight, and the ship was shrouded in thick rabbit-grey swirls. Peering through the fog, Malachi could see that the pirates were already up and about; and he could see why.

The other ship was now fully inside the

bottle, defensively positioned in the neck. It was smaller and darker than his ship; its sails and rigging dirty brown, its deck ebony, its cannons gleaming black.

Several sailors were scattered on the new ship's decks. They were better dressed than the pirates, with glints of gold sparking from their throats, ears and teeth. They also appeared unfazed, as if being face to face with another, heavily armed ship with a skull and crossbones flapping provocatively from its mast was the most natural thing in the world.

The new ship was also flying a flag. It was red, with a white heart and a dagger blazoned in its centre. But Malachi was not fooled. This new lot were pirates too, and they meant business.

On board his ship, numerous small hatches had opened in the hull, and its sides now bristled with cannons. There were twenty down each side, with six in the stern and six more mounted on the forecastle: fifty-two in all. All the pirates were also heavily armed, with cutlasses, pistols and hatchets crammed in their braces, belts and boots. They had already taken up their fighting positions: in the rigging, beside the cannons, or at the railings, grappling hooks clutched in their grimy fists.

All, that is, except three. The stowaway, red bandanna pirate and the pirate in the dirty jerkin were no longer on the ship. Instead, they were seated in a small skiff, and were rowing away from their ship. Were they running away? It seemed a very un-pirate-like thing to do. Malachi was surprised at their cowardice.

He turned the bottle around to get a better view of the skiff. If its three occupants were escaping, they weren't doing a very good job of it. They had rowed out into full view of the other ship, the stowaway perched in the bow making come-and-get-me gestures. What's more, in the bottom of the skiff was a treasure chest. Its lid was open, and jewels, goblets, golden chains and coins spewed from its top.

Really, thought Malachi, *they're asking for trouble.*

Then it dawned on him that being pursued was exactly what they wanted. The pirates in the skiff weren't running away at all. They were creating a decoy, hoping to lure their rivals away, so their shipmates could escape. They were being smart and bold, not cowardly. Smart, bold and exceptionally brave, when you considered how many cannons were ranged along the other ship's side, all pointing their way.

Malachi switched his attention to the other ship. It too had a figurehead, but unlike the graceful lady who fronted his ship, this one was squat and dark. Curled in upon herself, she hunched miserably under the bowsprit, draped in a hairy cape. Looking closer, Malachi realised the figure wasn't a lady at all, but an ape, its face contorted in a thin-lipped snarl beneath mean red eyes.

Malachi shuddered. Behind him, the sound of vigorous snuffling announced that piglet was awake and looking for something to eat. Malachi placed the ship in a bottle carefully on top of the piano, and jumped back to the floor. He reached through the bars to scratch piglet's head, stepping back rapidly when it bared its yellow teeth.

"Ow!" he said, as his thigh rammed into something hard. It was Mrs Green's machine.

The machine was the size of a small dishwasher. A large red lever – the cause of his sore leg – protruded from one side. A tangle of copper pipes ran down the other. The machine's body was completely swathed in bubble wrap, but a panel of multi-coloured knobs and buttons was still visible, ranged along the top.

Malachi pushed the red lever down. It swung easily. Nothing happened. He lifted it back up. This time there was an accompanying hiss. He swung the lever up and down a couple more times and the hiss started building steadily. Malachi jiggled the lever, trying to make the hissing stop, but it grew stronger and louder, until the machine began to vibrate.

"Uh oh," said Malachi. He punched at the row of buttons: red, green, pink, orange. A high-pitched beeping joined the hiss, then an insidious whine.

"Shh," said Malachi. "Shh. They'll find me."

The machine started rocking crazily, shuddering from side to side on its metal legs.

In desperation, Malachi grabbed one of the copper pipes and pulled. It came away, bringing with it a mess of raw wire. The machine juddered, beeped, hissed feebly and stopped.

Malachi slumped against piglet's cage in relief. With shaking hands, he reached for his water bottle, but froze when the bolt on the trailer's door started grinding open.

The Jarrods! They'd come. Now they would find him!

A puddle of cold water seeping around his toes brought Malachi to his senses. It was his water bottle; he'd knocked it over.

The truck doors came unstuck with a graunch and Malachi ducked. Scooping up the now empty water bottle, he tunnelled back through the trailer, reaching the sanctuary of the sofa just in time.

Chapter twenty

MR DOBBS GLOWERED into the trailer. He did not look like he had slept well. His face was a tepid shade of lilac, and a grizzle of whiskers shadowed his cheeks and chin. Angry creases etched his cheeks, as if his face had settled that way overnight and was proving sluggish to budge. He opened his mouth, gulped like a fish and bellowed. "Jarrod! Get here now, Jarrod!"

Jarrod, who had been hovering just out of sight, appeared at Mr Dobbs' elbow. He looked only marginally better than his father. Malachi wondered where they'd spent the night.

"Get in the back and check out that darned pig," Mr Dobbs said. "It's making a racket."

Jarrod clambered unsteadily onto the tailgate and edged his way towards the cage. Piglet's ears lay back along its skull. For every step Jarrod took towards it, piglet took one back, until it was wedged into the far corner of its cage. Its snout curled and it began to squeal.

"Dad, there's water …" Jarrod began.

"Don't be stupid, Jarrod. Pigs drink water."

"But outside the cage. There's a puddle."

Mr Dobbs scratched his head. "It's not that contraption of your teacher's, is it? It's not sprung a leak? Looks bleedin' expensive to me. She won't be happy if we break it."

He placed his palms on the tailgate and, after several noisy grunts, heaved himself into the trailer. Ignoring the piglet, he knelt next to its cage and stuck his finger in the puddle spilt from Malachi's water bottle.

"No idea where that's come from," he said, squinting at Mrs Green's machine, then around the trailer.

Malachi crouched as far into the cushion as he could go. Luckily, the pipe he'd pulled off was out of sight, on the machine's other side.

Mr Dobbs straightened up. "Sure stinks in here. I reckon that bleedin' pig's been sick. You can clean it up once we're shot of it, and I'll charge it to Flint. I'll take it off his bleedin' cut."

Still grumbling, he started to squeeze back past piglet's cage. Halfway along, he stopped. "What the heck?" he said, reaching over and picking up the ship in a bottle from the top of the piano.

Malachi stifled a groan. He had forgotten about the bottle.

"Well, I'll be darned," said Mr Dobbs.

"Where'd this come from?"

"What is it?" asked Jarrod.

His father held up the bottle. "A ship in a bottle. Actually, two ships. Now that's unusual. I've never seen two before."

"Is that where the water came from?" asked Jarrod.

"Don't be an idiot, Jarrod," said Mr Dobbs. "They don't put real water in them. They're just for display. They can be worth a fair bit, though, especially the old ones. I don't recall anyone putting it in, do you? One of those blighters probably thought they could slip it in for free."

Jarrod was hopping up and down, trying to get a good look at the ship.

"What ya gonna do with it?" he asked.

"Dunno," said Mr Dobbs.

"We could flog it," Jarrod said. "Claim we never saw it."

His father cuffed him on the ear, but for the

first time since they'd set off, Malachi saw him smile.

"If no one owns up, then we might just do that," he said. "Unlike that other rubbish Flint's had us collecting, this might actually be worth something." And with the smile still on his face, Mr Dobbs jumped down from the back of the trailer and with both hands slammed the doors shut.

Chapter twenty-one

MALACHI SPENT THE MORNING lying on the sofa in despair, as the truck bounced along an endless maze of pothole-pocked back roads picking up and delivering goods. Not only did he have no food and no water, he'd also lost the only important, if not exactly useful, thing he'd brought with him – the ship.

By the time the truck stopped mid-morning, Malachi was too down in the dumps to care where they were.

"It's a dark, dark day, piggy," he said, as he watched Jarrod and his father amble across the yard for their third cup of tea of the morning. Piglet gave a consoling grunt.

"You're right," said Malachi, hauling himself upright. "Lying around feeling sorry for ourselves isn't going to fix anything. What we need is to be smart like those pirates. What we need is a plan."

Piglet grunted again and Malachi crouched next to its cage. He reached in and scratched piglet's head. Piglet looked up at him forlornly.

"Actually, my friend," said Malachi, "I think I've got an idea, and the good news is it involves you. How brave are you feeling this morning?" He eased up the bolts on the cage door. Piglet got to its feet and grunted loudly. "Shhh," said Malachi. "We've got to wait for the right moment."

They didn't have to wait long. Five minutes later, Jarrod and his father stepped out of the tea hut. When he saw them, Malachi swung the cage door open. Piglet trotted to the tailgate and looked expectantly back at Malachi.

"Off you go then," said Malachi. "If you hang around here, you'll end up as Christmas dinner."

He gave piglet's rump a shove and it jumped off the tailgate and started trotting across the yard.

"I'd go a bit faster if I were you, piggy," Malachi muttered. But he needn't have worried. There was a bellow as Mr Dobbs noticed the escaped piglet, then both the Jarrods started running towards it, flailing their arms and yelling.

The effect was exactly as Malachi had planned. The panicked piglet, seeing the Jarrods coming, squealed and ran the opposite way. Other drivers, alerted by the commotion, joined the chase. More drivers came out of the smoko hut to see what was going on. Soon, they were all running around the yard, shouting, cursing and tripping over each other as they tried to round up the frightened piglet.

Malachi waited until the mob had piglet backed into the yard's far corner, before he slipped off the tailgate and moved stealthily down the side of the truck. He flicked open the cab door and slid in.

The cab was even more of a mess than when they had set off. There was stuff everywhere – drink bottles, food wrappers, loading slips and addresses – but there was no sign of the ship. Malachi sifted through piles of bags, clothes and papers, but he didn't find the bottle.

Outside, piglet had broken out of its corner and there was a fresh wave of shouting. The mob was heading his way. Malachi pulled the cab door shut behind him just as piglet sprinted past, followed closely by a posse of yelling drivers.

Feet thundered around the cab, as piglet

went first one way, then the other, trying to escape. Malachi flattened himself into the seat. If the Jarrods spotted him, he hated to think what they would do.

He was so busy imagining his unhappy fate that it was several moments before he realised the stampeding horde had gone. Piglet had escaped again, leading the chase back down the far end of the yard.

This was his chance. He had to get out of here, and quick. He scanned the cab once more, desperately hoping to locate the ship. It wasn't there, although he spotted something else.

In the middle of the back wall of the cab, there was a small sliding door. It was designed so whoever was riding upfront in the cab could check on things in the back. Malachi was amazed he hadn't noticed it before. It must open straight into the wall above the sofa where he'd been lying. If he'd known it was there, he'd have felt decidedly less safe.

Reaching up, he slid his fingers along the ledge until he found the latch. He flipped it up, and was about to test the door when there was renewed yelling from the far end of the yard. Malachi raised his head just in time to see piglet sprinting out of the yard gates, with the mob of drivers in hot pursuit.

It was like watching the tide rush out between rocks; one minute the truck yard was full of wild swirling noise, the next it was empty.

"Good on ya piggy. I owe you one," said Malachi.

He opened the cab door, slithered out and lowered himself to the ground. As he did, he noticed Mr Dobbs' cell phone on the cab floor by the door.

"Think I'll have that too," Malachi said. "You may have my ship, but I've got your phone. Think I could do with making a call."

The yard was empty. All the drivers had followed piglet up the road. The ground was strewn with sticks, tea cups and odd shoes, abandoned during the chase. Someone had dumped a blue plastic box next to a nearby truck. It could have been a toolbox, but a piece of greaseproof paper sticking out from under the lid suggested otherwise. As far as Malachi was concerned, greaseproof paper could only mean one thing.

He dashed across the yard and grabbed the box. Then, cell phone clutched in one hand and blue box in the other, he scuttled back to the safety of the trailer, where, with his back propped against piglet's cage, he opened his stolen treasure.

Chapter twenty-two

INSIDE THE BOX was everything Malachi could have hoped for. There were two paper-wrapped bundles of sandwiches, three hard-boiled eggs with a twist of salt, two apples, a piece of cake, crackers and cheese, a banana, and, tucked down one side, a sausage roll. The top of the box lifted off and underneath was a large bottle of water and a bar of chocolate.

Malachi found it difficult to savour his stolen lunch though, with piglet's fate uncertain and the ship in a bottle still missing.

If the Jarrods had taken the bottle with them to the tea hut, they may already have sold it. Even though he'd had it only a short while, the thought of being without it was hard to bear. Especially since the new ship had arrived and he'd witnessed the three pirates' bold bid to lure it away, Malachi had begun to see his ship and its motley crew in a much more favourable light.

"The Bold Ship Phenomenal," he muttered to himself. That was an altogether better name for the ship. A name fit for adventure, with a suitably daring ring to it.

Malachi gathered his things and pushed himself up off the trailer's floor. He didn't have the ship, but he still had its log. He'd change the name now, while he waited for piglet to return – the *Bold Ship Phenomenal*.

After half an hour, triumphant voices could be heard returning down the road. Soon after, piglet appeared at the tailgate, bundled between Jarrod and two drivers. Mr Dobbs manhandled it back into its cage, fastened the cage door with an enormous padlock and pocketed the key.

"Like to see you get out of that," he said, kicking the bars. "Need a cuppa after that run around. You coming, Jarrod?"

When the noise outside had settled down, Malachi sidled up to piglet's cage. Piglet had dropped spread-eagled onto the straw. It was even muddier than before, and had a couple of small cuts on its back legs.

"Still friends?" asked Malachi. Piglet gave him a mournful look. "Sorry about the chase," said Malachi. "But I'm about to make it up to you." He pushed an egg, an apple and a sandwich through the gap at the bottom of the cage. "Don't gulp your food though, you'll get indigestion."

The Jarrods returned and the truck set off once more. Piglet grunted contentedly in his cage and Malachi lay on his back and smiled at the ceiling, as they continued their journey north, this time with full stomachs.

Chapter twenty-three

UNTIL HE TRIED IT, Malachi never realised how hard it was to make a phone call in the dark, in the back of a truck, when every few seconds you're being jounced and jostled, up, down and side to side.

He'd ummed and ahhhed about whether to make the call at all. He wasn't in the most law-abiding position himself, and other than some royal jelly, his evidence wasn't particularly compelling. But in the end he decided he had to, if only for Jarrod's sake. Even so, it took him several attempts to punch in the numbers he needed, and then it was difficult to hear the emergency services operator over the noise of the engine.

"Police," he yelled, as loud as he could, before remembering the hatch above his head.

Then, when the operator did finally put him through to the Northland police, he'd tried to explain his situation.

"So where are you now?" the police officer asked.

"Somewhere up north," said Malachi.

"What do you mean by 'somewhere'?" asked the officer.

"We're heading for Omapere," said Malachi.

"And when do you expect to arrive?"

"Ahhh."

"Well, where did the robbery take place?"

"Ahhh."

"You did say they were stealing, didn't you?"

"Yes," said Malachi. "Truck piracy, and they're planning to do it again. A big job. Up north."

"Where exactly up north?"

"Ummm … not sure. They didn't say. It might have been Dargaville, but I let the pig out."

"Is it pigs they're stealing," asked the officer.

"No, trucks. I mean from trucks. But one of them is only a boy, it's his father who's making him do it."

"Did he tell you that?" asked the officer.

"Not exactly. He doesn't know I'm here."

"I thought you said you were in their truck."

"I am, but …"

"Look, son," the officer interrupted. "Up north is a big place. Why don't you ring me when you arrive? In the meantime, how about I give your parents a ring? I take it they know where you are?"

"Ummm."

"They know you're in this truck?"

"Ahh, I think I'll ring you back, like you say, once I get there," said Malachi, and he ended the call. Then he turned the phone off. The last thing he wanted was for the police to track him down and take him home, before he'd even arrived at the place he wanted to go.

Malachi spent the rest of the afternoon lying on the sofa staring at the ceiling, as the truck bumped and wound its way north.

The Jarrods were gradually despatching the items they'd picked up the day before. The loom, chafe separator and worm farm were all unloaded at farms along the way, Jarrod struggling to get them out of the trailer while Mr Dobbs made vigorous ticks on his clipboard. When the car bonnet was unloaded, Malachi's torch rolled out from underneath it, and when the Jarrods went for yet another cup of tea, Malachi grabbed it. The lens had broken, but the bulb still worked.

By early afternoon, only piglet, Mrs Green's machine, the stolen royal jelly and the sofa were left. Malachi felt sure they must be nearly there.

Piglet, too, seemed aware that something was up, and was curled in a woeful ball in the corner of its cage. When they reached Flint's daughter's house, however, there was no one home to claim it.

"Darn that Flint," said Mr Dobbs. "He said they'd be here. Get the phone, Jarrod. I'll give him a call, find out what he's up to."

Jarrod trotted off, returning a few minutes later empty handed. "Can't find it," he said.

"What do mean you can't find it? It's on the floor of the bleedin' cab where it always is."

"I looked," said Jarrod. "It's not there now."

His father stomped off, but was soon back. "Well you can darn well find it when we get there," he said. "We're gonna need it so Blacko can phone us about the drop." He glowered at piglet's cage. "We'll just have to take that dratted animal with us. And I'll ring Flint tonight and tell him if his sister isn't here when we make the home run, we're gonna eat the darned thing ourselves."

Malachi was glad piglet was still on board. He had grown quite fond of it. Piglet, too, seemed pleased to be there, grunting appreciatively as Malachi shared his sausage roll and the remainder of the sandwiches.

The next leg of the journey was the worst yet. From the map, Malachi had assumed the final run to Omapere would be smooth sailing. Instead, it was as if the truck was under fire. Loud crashes and bangs ricocheted off the roof and floor, while groans and grinds imploded within the walls. At times, the wheels hit potholes so deep that the legs of the sofa left the ground.

Malachi kept his head low for fear of being struck by flying objects. At one point, his backpack was thrown the length of the trailer.

He crawled after it, finding it by feeling about in the dark. The cell phone had gone from the outside pocket, and although he hunted for another five minutes, Malachi couldn't find it.

As he was crawling back to the sofa, the truck hit another huge hole and Malachi was flung painfully against the wall. Where on earth were they? They should be on State Highway 12 by now, and surely, even this far north, it should be tarseal. Instead, he could have sworn they were crossing an open field. Yet Mr Dobbs showed no signs of stopping, gunning the engine at every impact and revving around corners and up hills, until, with a final groan, the truck ground to a juddering halt.

Chapter twenty-four

MALACHI COULDN'T BELIEVE his eyes. He blinked, closed them, counted to twenty, then blinked again, before looking once more out of the trailer's back door.

But the sign still said the same thing.

Waipoua Forest
Department of Conservation Research Centre
Staff only beyond this point

Not Omapere after all, but the best possible destination. And not just the best possible destination, but the best possible spot, at the best possible destination.

Beyond the sign, Malachi could see a wooden gate, and beyond that a dirt road leading into the forest. The Jarrods had already disappeared down it. Maybe they had something to pick up? Malachi no longer cared. He had some protestors to find.

A loud snort interrupted Malachi's thoughts. Piglet was pushing its snout through the bars of its cage.

"Sorry piggy, this is where I get out," Malachi said, scratching the wrinkled nose. "I'd take you with me, but they've locked you in. You'll just have to try and escape when you get there. Make sure you do it before Christmas, though."

He pushed the remains of the driver's lunch through the bars and stepped onto the tailgate.

Everywhere he looked there were trees. Elegant elongated ones whose tops disappeared into the canopy, and enormous squat ones, with ample grandmotherly girths and a patient, steadfast air. Slender saplings sheltered at their feet, spindly limbs thrust towards the light.

After the hubbub of the truck yards, the forest seemed oddly quiet. Yet the air trembled with green energy, vibrating to the run of sap and the passage of the trees' collective breath. Malachi stretched his own arms high above his head and breathed deeply. Finally he had arrived.

Amongst the green, a flash of red caught his eye. It was Jarrod, slouching along the dirt road, eyes fixed on his shoes. As he reached the gate, he glanced up.

Malachi bolted. He leapt back into the trailer and commando rolled over the top of the sofa. As he hit the cushion, he realised his mistake.

If he'd jumped out and run, Jarrod would never have caught him. Now he was cornered, and somehow he doubted either Jarrod or his father would be pleased to see him.

Chapter twenty-five

"HEY, HEY YOU," Jarrod shouted. The whole truck bounced as he hurled himself onto the tailgate. "What the … where the … I know you're …"

Jarrod took a couple of steps into the gloom. Malachi held his breath.

"Whoever you are, you'd better come out," Jarrod said loudly. "If my father finds out that you've been …"

At the mention of Jarrod's father, piglet

started to squeak: a string of small shrill notes that within seconds blossomed into squeals. Jarrod kicked its cage.

"Shut up you stupid animal. You'll get it too, if you don't shut your trap."

Piglet squealed louder. Malachi put his hands over his ears as Jarrod grabbed hold of the cage and started shaking it.

"Shut up, SHUT UP! I'm going to stuff your mouth and make you into bacon if you don't …"

"Jarrod!" Mr Dobbs bellowed so loudly that both Jarrod and piglet froze. "What on earth are you doing to that bleedin' pig?"

"D-D-Dad," Jarrod stammered. "I-I-I saw … there was someone … I thought they … b-b-but now it's empty … in the bush … they must be in the bush."

"For cripes' sake, Jarrod, you're blabbering like a baby. Who's in the bush?"

"A person. He was standing …"

"People do."

147

"In the truck."

"Someone was in the truck?" Mr Dobbs went purple in the face. "Who?"

"I dunno. I saw him, then he was gone. I thought he must have got in the back, but there's no one there now. He must have run into the bush."

"Huh." Mr Dobbs glanced into the trailer. "Probably one of those hippy types. What did he look like? Big guy?"

"No, sort of weedy. Actually, he looked a bit like a kid from school."

"Don't be ridiculous, Jarrod. What would a kid from your school be doing all the way up here?"

Jarrod kicked the gravel. "I didn't say it was him. I said it looked like him."

"We'll have to be careful," said Mr Dobbs. "There might still be a few of those hippies hanging around. They might be on to us."

"So what do we do now?" asked Jarrod.

"We find out where this contraption is going. Then we wait until we hear from Blacko, give it half an hour, collect the cages and split. Simple."

"But what will be in them?" asked Jarrod.

"Animals, of course," said Mr Dobbs. "Kiwi, gecko, tui. You should have seen the size of the snail I picked up once." He balled his hand into a fist. "I swear it was that big."

Snails! Malachi sat bolt upright and glared at the Jarrods over the top of the sofa. They were planning on nicking his science project. He had to stop them. Then he realised what he was doing and lay quickly back down.

"But those animals belong in the forest," said Jarrod. "Some of them are protected. You can't just take them out of it."

Malachi felt a twinge of remorse. Jarrod was right. If he, Malachi, took a snail for his project, he'd be no better than them.

"Collectors pay good money for those

animals," said Mr Dobbs. "It's not up to us to say if it's right or wrong. We're just the purveyors. Piratical purveyors of rare goods for those that want them and have got the cash to pay. Besides, the animals will be looked after. Either that or stuffed." He cackled. Jarrod winced. "Now you wait here," he continued. "I'll sort out where this load is going. Then we'll shift it."

"What if the hippy comes back?" said Jarrod.

"Tell him to stuff off."

"Right. Stuff off," Jarrod repeated, but he didn't sound very sure.

"And Jarrod?"

"Yep?"

"Leave the pig alone."

Chapter twenty-six

JARROD SAT ON THE TAILGATE and stared morosely at his knees. He looked younger somehow, more like the boy he was, and less like the swaggering bully he seemed at school.

Malachi felt sorry for him, but he couldn't help him now. It was more important that he stopped Mr Dobbs getting his hands on those animals. For that, he'd need back-up: if the police wouldn't help him, the protestors would.

But first he had to find a way to get past

Jarrod and out of the truck. He could make a run for it, but Jarrod was twice his size and he didn't fancy his chances. Even if he did manage to dodge him, there was no way he'd get away unrecognised a second time. If the Jarrods knew he was loose in the forest, it would be him they'd be hunting, not the animals.

After a short while, Mr Dobbs came back. "What are you sitting there for?" he asked Jarrod. "You should be looking for that bleedin' phone."

Jarrod stumbled to his feet. "I was waiting for you."

"Well don't wait. We haven't got all bleedin' day, and what's-her-name is fluffing around about what she wants doing with that darned contraption. I told her we'd unload it and get it down the track, then she can do what she darn well likes with it. Better get that pig out too, so we can stash the animals behind it. We'll have to cover their cages, in case we get stopped."

For ten minutes the truck reverberated to grunting, cursing and metal scraping against metal. When the din stopped and Malachi felt it was safe to look, Mrs Green's machine had gone. Piglet's cage had also been unloaded and placed at the edge of the car park in the shade. Both the Jarrods were leaning on it, sweat dripping from their chins.

"What the heck?" Mr Dobbs squinted down into piglet's cage. He got down on his knees and reached through the bars. "It's the bleedin' cell phone," he said. "You must have left it there."

"Didn't," said Jarrod. "Maybe it was the hippy."

"You think the hippy stole the phone and gave it to the pig?" Mr Dobbs threw the phone at Jarrod. Jarrod caught it just in time. "Turn it on. See if it still works."

Jarrod did as he was told. "Seems to," he said.

"Leave it on for Blacko then," said his father.

"And go and look in the cab, make sure that hippy hasn't got his mitts on anything else."

Jarrod pouted sulkily. "Why don't you do it?"

"Because I'm going to check in the back, make sure he hasn't planted a tracking device or something. They may be on to us."

Malachi pressed so hard into the sofa he felt as if he was spreading sideways. This was definitely the end of the road. In a few seconds, Mr Dobbs would be leaning over him, and it wouldn't matter how flat he felt, there'd be nowhere to run.

His breath rasped in his throat and his eyes stung. On one side he could hear Jarrod rummaging in the cab, and on the other, Mr Dobbs, muttering by the tailgate, preparing to climb in. Malachi was so gripped by terror and frustration that he barely flinched when someone shouted right next to his ear.

But it was Jarrod, not his father, who'd

shouted, and moments later he reappeared outside the truck, clutching something in his hands. The bottle!

"Well I'll be blowed,' said Mr Dobbs. "Where'd you find that?"

"Under the seat, where you stashed it. What's happened to it?"

"Darned if I know," said Mr Dobbs, taking the bottle off Jarrod. "Can't see a darned thing, there's so much smoke. Can't even see the ships."

"Maybe the hippy burned them," said Jarrod.

"Why would he do that?" said Mr Dobbs.

Jarrod shrugged. "To give us a scare. Warn us not to take the animals."

His father glared at him. "Well it's not going to work, is it?" He placed the bottle inside the trailer. "We can deal with that later. Right now we've got a delivery to make, and after that, some loot to collect. So get busy and load that contraption on the trolley while I find out where we're taking it. Oh, and I guess we'd better shut up the truck in case that hippy decides to meddle with something else. You get the cab. I'll get the back."

And as Malachi watched, Mr Dobbs slammed and bolted the trailer's doors with a series of resounding clunks.

Chapter twenty-seven

As soon as the Jarrods were gone, Malachi vaulted over the back of the sofa and crawled around on his hands and knees until he found the bottle.

The glass was oddly hot, but seemed to be unharmed. He couldn't tell what was happening inside though. When he stood on tiptoes and held the bottle towards the meagre light filtering through the ventilation slits, all he could see was a dense blanket of dirty smoke. But he had the bottle back, that was what counted, and he handled it with extra care as he stowed it securely in the top of his pack.

What now? Here he was in the Waipoua Forest. The beginning of his adventure was mere metres from where he sat. Yet he was no closer to having it than he had been at home. What's more, the Jarrods were out there, stealing animals, committing a crime, and he had no way of stopping them. He should have run while he could. Now he was locked in – again.

Malachi felt like crying, but his eyes were dry as raisins. Instead he raised his fist and slammed it on the wall above his head. It hurt, so he did it again, harder. He was so annoyed – at himself, his father, the stupid truck, Jarrod and his swaggering dad. He was even annoyed at the protestors for choosing this out-of-the-way place to protest, and at his mother for raising him to think adventure was a good thing in the first place. He'd know better in future.

Malachi hit the truck wall again. This time his fist grazed something blunt sticking out from the wall. "Ow!" he said. He sucked his grazed knuckles. What had he hit?

He knelt on the sofa and inched his palms up the wall until his fingers found a narrow ledge. He slid his hands higher, feeling out a small oblong recess.

"Way to go piggy," he said, before he remembered that piglet was now outside the truck. "I'll be with you soon," he added.

Standing on the sofa, Malachi leaned into the recess and shoved. The hatch door was stiff at first, but then slid easily. There was only a small opening, designed for looking, not climbing through. For the first time in his life, Malachi was pleased he was skinny.

Pushing his backpack in front of him, he wiggled and squirmed until first his shoulders, then his ribs were through. His hips grated against the ledge as he pulled himself into the cab, but Malachi didn't care. This time there was no going back. This time he really had arrived.

Chapter twenty-eight

MALACHI CROUCHED IN the undergrowth. He'd considered heading into the forest, but didn't want to bump into the Jarrods, so instead hid behind an enormous log and waited for them to return.

Next to him, the neck of the bottle stuck out from the top of his backpack. It was filled with thick smoke, and when he touched it, the glass was still warm. Finding out what was causing the heat would have to wait though. He couldn't risk undoing his backpack now, when at any moment he may have to flee.

Mr Dobbs appeared first, striding out of the forest, clipboard in hand. When he saw the truck, he stopped.

"I thought I told you to lock the cab," he yelled at Jarrod who was trotting behind.

"I-I-I did," Jarrod stammered.

"Obviously you bleedin' didn't," said his father, pointing to the wide-open cab door. "Now those hippies have been in again and who knows what they've taken. We're lucky they didn't take the jolly truck." Mr Dobbs swung his clipboard at Jarrod, who ducked away just in time.

Malachi turned his back on them and crept off through the undergrowth. He wished he'd thought to close the door behind him when he'd made his escape, but there was nothing he could do about that now. He had to get to the protestors, before the Jarrods got to the animals.

Somehow he thought Jarrod would understand.

Once he was away from the car park, it was surprisingly hard to know which way to go. He decided to cut diagonally towards the dirt road, but the forest was denser than it looked from its fringes, and it was difficult, when all he could see was trees, to know if he was heading in a straight line.

A couple of times he struck out towards a lighter area, thinking it might be the road, only to find a fallen tree had left a gap in the canopy. Eventually, though, a glint of metal caught his eye. He thrashed his way towards it and stumbled out of the undergrowth and into a clearing, with the dirt road just visible beyond.

Malachi recognised the place immediately. It was the protestors' camp he'd seen on TV. Or at least, what used to be their camp – a large flat area of dirt and bush surrounding an olive-green research centre hut.

Further down the dirt road, Malachi could

see the wooden gate leading to the car park. The camp couldn't be more than one hundred metres away from the car park, yet it had taken him over an hour to find it.

Malachi gazed numbly from the hut to the gate to the trees and back again. If he'd known how close the car park was to the campsite, he might have been suspicious. He might have wondered why he couldn't hear voices or drums, why no one appeared, why there were no cars parked alongside the truck.

But he hadn't known and his mind had been on other things. Now he did.

The protest was over, and every last protestor had upped camp and gone away.

Chapter twenty-nine

MALACHI STUMBLED AROUND the empty campsite. The undergrowth around the hut had been trampled into a warren of narrow paths. There were clearings where people had gathered, and beaten yellowed areas where tents had stood. Logs had been arranged into companionable circles, and makeshift shelters fashioned from branches and ferns. There were ghosts of smells too – incense, canvas, camp smoke, bacon – but not a sign of the people who'd made them. Not so much as a sweet wrapper marred the forest floor. The hut was locked, its windows barred, a bolt and padlock secured its door.

If Malachi had thought the forest quiet before, he didn't now. Small birds warbled and tui croaked. Branches creaked, leaves rustled, insects chirruped. There were rumours of trapped breezes and secretive water, of gradual shedding and even more gradual earthy shifting. It was as if the whole forest was suddenly on stereo to emphasise the sound Malachi couldn't hear – human voices.

He circled round to the front of the hut and stopped. Here, someone had left something behind.

Rising from the forest floor like a massive tropical flower, was the totem pole he'd seen on TV. It was even more colourful and fantastical than it had looked on screen, the wood alive with carved and painted plants and animals.

Across its top, four large metal blades splayed, forming an enormous silver cross. The blades were wing-shaped, with feathered edges and delicate tips, and swayed gently in the breeze.

Malachi laid his hand on the pole's base. Next to his palm, a dark green lizard scaled a carved branch, creeping towards a fantail perched just beyond Malachi's fingertips. Above it, a kereru peered haughtily down from amongst a wreath of puriri flowers, while a rosella swooped in a blaze of colour down the opposite side of the pole. At his feet, a hedgehog and a rat scuffled around the pole's base, towards a large circular carving: a stone or an egg.

Malachi hunkered down for a closer look. The slightly off-kilter circle had a delicate koru carved on its face and was neither stone nor egg. It was a shell … a snail shell.

"Pupurangi," whispered Malachi, tracing the shell's curve with his fingers. "X marks the spot."

He'd found the right spot all right, but he was too late. Why had the protestors gone, and where to? Had the police forced them out? And why had the Jarrods unloaded Mrs Green's machine here? Was she part of their smuggling ring? A more likely explanation was that she was in cahoots with the council, gathering evidence to prosecute the protestors. Malachi wished he'd known. He would have carried out some more lasting sabotage on that machine of hers – a small protest of his own.

Chapter thirty

MALACHI SAT WITH his back propped against the pole, his bag in his lap. What now? How could he take on the Jarrods alone, without the protestors' help? And how could he ever find the stolen animals amongst this endless procession of trees?

His legs were hot and he shifted them into the shade. But the heat intensified, until it broke through his thoughts, and he realised it was the bottle that was burning him and not the sun.

Malachi pulled it out of the bag.

The smoke had cleared, and inside the bottle a battle was underway. Cannons fired, sparks flew and the sea broiled with misfired shots, dislodged cargo and floundering pirates.

At the *Bold Ship Phenomenal*'s helm, the stowaway had a blunderbuss propped against his shoulder, aimed at the other ship. All that now separated the two hulls was a ribbon of murky sea. Sandwiched between them, in the skiff, the red bandanna pirate was locked in mortal combat with a burly pirate from the other crew. Red bandanna swung a club wildly, as the other pirate grappled to get him in a head lock, grimacing grimly through blackened teeth.

"Get away," hissed Malachi, but nobody moved.

On board the *Bold Ship Phenomenal*, clusters of pirates raced to reload the cannons. Tendrils of smoke trickled from the cannons' black mouths. It must have been billows from the battle's opening volleys that had earlier filled the bottle. Whatever the cause, that smoke had saved Malachi's adventure, if not his life, diverting Mr Dobbs as he was about to discover his hiding place.

Something moved, but it was outside the bottle, not in. Jarrod and his father were coming around the hut towards the pole.

Malachi was on his feet, bag under one arm, bottle under the other, bolting for the cover of the forest, by the time they spotted him.

"It's the hippy! It's the hippy!" Jarrod yelled, as Malachi crashed into the undergrowth beneath the trees.

"After him!" yelled Mr Dobbs. But Malachi had got a head start. The Jarrods struck off to the left, while Malachi ducked under a fallen branch and headed right. He could hear them cursing and yelling, but the forest was too deeply shadowed and they didn't spot him.

Their voices grew fainter and fainter, until he couldn't hear them at all.

Malachi kept going, pushing his way between the scrub and vines, desperate to put as much distance as possible between himself and the Jarrods. After what seemed an age, he came to a narrow path and stopped, unsure whether to take it. If he did, he would be travelling in the open, away from the shelter of the trees. It would be easier than pushing through the bush, though, and he was beginning to feel weary.

As he hesitated, his decision was made for him. The Jarrods came lumbering out of the trees a short distance away. They were puffing hard and staring at the cell phone clutched in Jarrod's hands.

"Get the map up then, Jarrod," said Mr Dobbs. "We need to find where he's stashed them before dark." Then he looked up.

Malachi turned and fled. He ignored the clawing branches and the thorns that snagged his clothes and bag. Coming to a swamp, he plunged straight through it, sinking to his knees in the black sulphurous mud. The Jarrods were close behind, and shouted angrily when they hit the mud. Malachi dodged away as they hunted for a way around.

This time he wasn't stopping. His legs and back ached, his eyes watered and his breath came in racking gulps. He had lost the Jarrods, but still he kept running, leaping logs and dodging roots and hidden hollows, until he plunged between two rimu and came up short against the enormous moss-covered trunk of a fallen kauri. The tree's bulk stretched into the undergrowth on either side, blocking his path as far as he could see. Malachi leaned against it, panting hard. He was too tired to carry on.

Chapter thirty-one

MALACHI CROUCHED IN THE LEE of the giant
fallen kauri. He may have evaded the Jarrods,
but he'd lost himself in the process. The fallen
tree was huge enough to be a landmark of sorts,
but a landmark was no use when he had no idea
where in the forest it, or he, was.

Malachi found its bulk comforting though.
Even lying on its side, the trunk towered above
his head. It formed a blockade between him and
the rest of the forest, hiding him from anyone

approaching on its other side, and was as good a spot as any to stop. The Jarrods would not hunt for him forever. He need only wait until they had made their pick-up and driven off, then he could search for a way out of this place.

He realised he was still clutching the ship in a bottle, and when he looked, he saw it had changed again during his flight.

The newcomers had now swung their ship sideways in the bottle, so it stood broadside to the *Bold Ship Phenomenal*. Its menacing hull was thick with cannons. The balance of the battle had also swung, and the new pirates crowded the railings of their ship, jeering as they made ready to board the *Bold Ship Phenomenal*, which was listing heavily as it tried to pull away.

His own pirates, as Malachi now thought of them, appeared panicked. Above their heads, several sails were on fire. The decks were strewn with dislodged cargo and debris, and pirates stumbled among the mess, many injured and no longer armed. Malachi could not immediately see the pirate with the red bandanna, but eventually located him on the forecastle of the enemy ship. His earlier skirmish had clearly not gone in his favour. His hands and feet were bound and the pirate with the black teeth stood behind him, his pistol cocked against his captive's ear.

Malachi needed to do something. He needed to save the pirate with the red bandanna and change the course of the battle. But how? Then he spotted the stowaway. He was climbing a rope, which he'd slung over the forecastle railing of the enemy ship. He was braced against the hull, arms and legs rigid with effort, his hands white upon the rope. Between his teeth was clenched a curved kopi dagger. Red bandanna's captor stood with his back to the railing, unaware that a rescue mission was underway.

Malachi shook the bottle up and down in excitement.

"Free him! Free him!" he yelled.

There was an answering yell behind his back.

"Did you hear that?" called the voice.

"Hear what?" answered a second voice.

Malachi froze. It was the Jarrods, on the other side of the fallen trunk.

"Someone yelled," said Mr Dobbs.

"It must be him," said Jarrod.

"He's close by," said Mr Dobbs. "Be quiet so I can listen."

Malachi held his breath. His knees shook and his palms slid with sweat against the bottle's sides. He could hear the Jarrods shuffling about on the other side of the trunk, then the shuffling stopped and everything went quiet. He dared not move. Perhaps they'd gone away?

"Got you!"

This time the yell was right above Malachi's head. He jumped up and dropped the bottle. Mr Dobbs was glaring down at him from the top of the fallen trunk, his face purple with rage. Jarrod's head popped up alongside.

"It's, it's, it's …" Jarrod spluttered.

Malachi picked up the bottle and ran.

"Stop him!" roared Mr Dobbs. "He's got our bottle."

Malachi glanced back to see Mr Dobbs sliding down the trunk behind him. Jarrod made to follow, but his foot snagged on a knot halfway down. He teetered, toppling slowly outwards, before plunging head first to the ground, knocking his father flat on the way.

"Ouch," said Malachi, suppressing a laugh. He took one last glance at the Jarrods sprawled on the forest floor, then, grabbing his bag and clutching the bottle, plunged into the trees once more.

Chapter thirty-two

MALACHI LEAPT, dodged, scaled, sidestepped, burrowed and crashed. Vines whipped his shins and roots trapped his toes. Twice he stumbled, the second time jarring his right wrist so badly that he cried out with pain. Yet he couldn't shake off the Jarrods, and the sound of their crashing and swearing followed him, like a bad-natured echo, through the bush.

He was almost too tired to carry on when he spotted another path. Gratefully, he took it, following its narrow passage until he reached a thick stand of punga.

The tree ferns' inky trunks made a pool of darker shadow within the dim undergrowth. Malachi veered off into them, heading for the gloomy heart of the stand where the shadows looked almost black. But when he reached it, he found the blackness wasn't shadows, it was a cave.

The cave was tucked under a low hillock and had a wide shallow mouth. Dead punga logs and fronds were piled around it. *Almost*, thought Malachi, *as if someone had tried to disguise the entrance.* He dropped to his knees and crawled inside, inching into the darkness until he was sure he couldn't be seen from outside.

The Jarrods soon reached the stand of punga. Malachi couldn't see them, but could hear their heavy breathing and plodding tread.

"It was him, Dad, it was," said Jarrod. "He's in my class."

"So what?" his father replied. "What's that got to do with the fact that he's got our bottle?"

"Maybe it's his bottle."

"How can it be his bottle? We found it fair and square in the back of our truck, so that makes it ours, and whether he's your bleedin' schoolmate or not, I want it back."

"Maybe he was in the truck too?" said Jarrod.

"Don't be stupid, Jarrod. Obviously she brought him up here with her. He must be helping her."

Jarrod's voice rose to a wail. "What if he knows about the animals? What if he overheard us?"

Mr Dobb's coughed up a mouthful of phlegm and spat it into the bush.

"What's he going to do? Call the police? Now stop your whinging and take another look at that damned phone. We've lost him, so we may as well find the animals. What do the coordinates say?"

"Don't know. I can't read it."

"What do you mean you can't read it? Don't they teach you anything at school? Here, give it to me."

Malachi sat like a stone until the Jarrods had passed. Even then he stayed where he was, too scared and exhausted to move. When his legs started to go numb beneath him, he shuffled to the mouth of the cave and checked on the bottle.

He was glad he had. Something strange and dramatic was happening inside. A huge wave curved the length of the bottle, towering above the small ships, which leaned at a perilous angle. Pirates, cargo and animals were hanging, swaying and sliding to one side, some plunging from the decks into the sea below.

From the forecastle of the enemy ship, the stowaway swung wildly on the end of his rope. Red bandanna pirate had toppled, still bound, onto his side and was bracing himself against the chests to prevent himself from being hurled into the sea. His captor was not so lucky. He was flying head first towards the water, his pistol still clutched in his hand and a surprised look upon his face.

Malachi knew exactly what had happened. His earlier excited shaking had created a rogue wave inside the bottle, taking everyone on board the ships by surprise. And he knew what he had to now do. The *Bold Ship Phenomenal* had saved him earlier from certain disaster. It was his turn to save it.

Grabbing the bottle with both hands, he began to shake it up and down, but that hurt his injured wrist, so he grabbed the bottle's neck with his left hand and swung it round and round above his head like a shot-put. What he needed was a storm: a tempest on the ocean, a hurricane on the high seas. Something with sufficient force to drive the two ships apart and expel the enemy pirates from the bottle.

Malachi swung the bottle until his arm ached. When he eventually stopped and looked inside, everything was the same. That didn't surprise him. He knew enough of the bottle's ways now to realise it wouldn't change while he watched it. He put it back in his pack, satisfied that when the time came, he would have created enough chaos inside to enable the *Bold Ship Phenomenal* to escape.

It was time to go. The Jarrods would be far enough ahead, and he needed to find his way back to the clearing before it got dtark. He started to crawl out of the cave, but stopped as a sudden chorus of bird calls erupted behind him: high urgent piping notes and sharp trills and squeaks. These calls weren't song, they were cries of fear and distress – and they were coming from the cave.

Chapter thirty-three

MALACHI TURNED SLOWLY AROUND. The bird calls peaked, then died away as suddenly as they had begun. There was no doubt, though, that they had come from the cave. The damp air hummed, even after they'd stopped.

Malachi edged his way back into the darkness. Not far beyond its mouth, the cave opened up, and he was soon able to get up off his knees and stand. He stepped forward slowly, keeping his hand on the cool rock wall to guide him. When his fingers touched metal, he jerked his hand back in surprise. There was a muffled squawk.

All Malachi could see were shades of dark: murky edges and corners, pale recesses and glints of light. He hunted in his pack for his torch, and flicked it on. Thankfully it still worked.

The cave sprung up around him. It wasn't large, and he'd already reached its back wall. Malachi gasped as he realised what he'd touched. The cave's back wall was covered in cages. They were stacked four and five high, their doors latched shut and secured with twine.

Malachi shone his torch over them. There was a stir of fluffing and rustling. The cages were full of birds. Tui and bellbirds, tom tits, wax eyes and kakariki. Two fat kereru huddled at the back of a small cage, while next to them, in a larger cage, several rosella clung to makeshift perches. One whistled plaintively.

Next to the cages was a pile of wooden boxes, all secured with heavy padlocks. Behind them were six more cages, covered with sacks. Malachi lifted a corner and saw the unmistakable feathered curve of a kiwi's back.

"This is terrible," he whispered.

Malachi had no doubt this was the loot the Jarrods had come to collect. There must have been hundreds of animals in the cave, all miserable and all destined for somewhere other than where they belonged. It was only a matter of time before the Jarrods worked out how to use the map on their phone and made their way back to find them. He had to get the animals out.

Malachi checked the kiwi cages first, but like the boxes, they were all padlocked shut. He tried to untie the twine on another cage, but his injured right hand hurt too much, and he had no success with his left. He thought of the stowaway scaling the rope with his dagger between his teeth. What he needed was something to cut the birds free with. He didn't have a dagger, but he did have his pocket knife. Like most of the things he'd packed for his journey, he hadn't needed it: until now.

Still, cutting the twine left-handed proved difficult and slow work. Malachi kept fumbling and dropping the knife, and every sound from the cages or forest made him jump and spin around, terrified the Jarrods had returned.

Eventually, though, all the twine was cut and he opened the cage doors wide. None of the birds moved. He reached into the nearest cage, but the tui inside panicked, beating its wings against the bars. He tried a cage of fantails, but they too fled to the back of the cage, open-beaked with terror. The kereru were easier. Their cage was too small for them to evade his hands, although they pecked at his wrist as he lifted them out.

He placed the birds on the floor, but whether

it was fright or the false twilight of the cave, they seemed reluctant to go. Malachi shooed them towards the cave mouth. They hopped nervously forward. Then, as soon as the first birds reached the light, they spread their wings and took flight.

It was as if he had opened a floodgate. There was a rush of wings behind him as flocks of birds left their cages and flew to freedom. He crawled outside to watch them go – flashes of black and blue, white, purple and green, rising past him and into the trees, like the sparks from a fantastical fire. Then they were gone.

Malachi went back into the cave. He shooed out a few stragglers, then turned his attention to the padlocks on the boxes. He wanted to see what was inside. Presumably the smaller reptiles and insects the Jarrods had talked about. Would there be a snail?

Malachi flicked the hoof-pick out on his knife. He'd attempted to pick locks with it before, with little success. This time was no different. The blade was too big for the lock, and kept slipping and stabbing his palm.

He picked up one of the boxes and moved it towards the cave mouth to give himself more light. Inside the box something scuttled, then stopped. Malachi placed the box carefully on the cave floor and had another look at the lock.

As he did so, a new sound wailed through the forest. It was familiar, but so totally out of place that it took Malachi a few moments to understand what it meant. Then he did and, leaving the box where it was, he grabbed his pack and his knife and once again started to run.

The new sound was the shrill whine of sirens, and it was coming from somewhere close by.

Chapter thirty-four

MALACHI RAN WITH ALL his might towards the sound of the sirens. He followed the narrow path that he'd run along before, no longer caring who he might bump into. After just a few minutes, the path joined up to the forest road, close to the wooden gate. For Malachi's hammering heart and exhausted legs it seemed to take forever.

Yet, when he finally lurched through the gate and out into the open in the car park, he was too late. Although he saw the policeman driving the police car down the gravel road out of the forest, with Jarrod and Mr Dobbs in the back, and although he also saw a second policeman following close behind at the wheel of Mr Dobbs' truck, none of them saw him.

Before he could think about shouting or waving to get their attention, both the car and the truck were gone. Only a drift of dust showed where they had been.

Malachi was alone, left behind in the forest. No protestors, no phone, no snail, no food – again! The things he lacked ran through his head like the chorus from a corny song.

Malachi no longer cared. Evening shadows were gathering like moths around him. All he had the energy to do was drop his backpack and spend the night sitting right where he was, on the gravel in the middle of the car park, until dawn came and he could walk to the main road and begin his long journey home.

Which was exactly what he intended to do, until his thoughts were interrupted by yet another sound. This time, Malachi was sure he'd imagined it. He thought nostalgically of his small lost friend; but wishing for something didn't make it real. Then he heard it again – that distinctive high-pitched squeal.

Malachi spun on his heel, trying to find where it was coming from. He spotted the cage first, then its occupant, just visible in the deepening gloom beneath the trees.

Piglet! Like Malachi, it had been left behind.

Chapter thirty-five

PIGLET STUCK ITS SNOUT through the bars of its cage. Malachi gave it a good scratch.

"No food, I'm afraid," he said. "But at least you've got a friend, and so have I. That's got to be worth something."

He settled himself on the ground next to the cage and, once piglet had settled down too, took out the ship in a bottle. Using his torch, he looked through the glass. Immediately, he wished he hadn't.

The *Bold Ship Phenomenal* was alone in the bottle. Parts of its hull had been blown away, revealing its ribs and spars, and beyond them, the grimy darkness of the hold. One of the cannons had been blasted clean from its place, and the others were inky with gunpowder. Remnants of cannon smoke loitered, turning in dirty curls around the remains of the sails, which hung from the masts in blackened shreds. One mast was broken and all of the cargo that had been stored on deck was shattered. Fragments of crates, straw and wadding spread from the ship's prow to its stern.

On the port side, a handful of dead rats floated in the water, while on the quarterdeck a sole pirate lay in a pool of plum-coloured blood. It was the pirate with the dirty jerkin. Red bandanna pirate and the stowaway were nowhere to be seen.

The enemy pirates had won. There was no sign of their ship now, not even a furrow in the waves where its hull had passed. They had fought to victory, plundered the *Bold Ship Phenomenal*, and left, taking the beautiful figurehead with them. The bowsprit she'd hung from was nothing more than a splintered stick.

At least, Malachi hoped they'd taken her with them. The alternative made him feel sick. He imagined the blast as the figurehead was hit by crossfire, the instant of stillness, then her plunge into the murderous sea. She would have floated at first, face turned mutely upwards, until gradually she surrendered to the sunless depths.

Malachi shuddered when he thought of the part he'd played in the pirates' downfall. He'd tried to raise a storm, but instead created carnage. Now the ship was wrecked and the pirates all gone: captured, deserted or dead.

He should never have interfered. His attempt to save the ship was just another failure in a journey that he now realised had been doomed from the start.

It was dark now. After half an hour of scuffling and tussling, the forest birds had settled to sleep. Only the moreporks still called as they winged their way upon the hunt. In the sky above the car park, a smattering of stars flickered. The trees around had flattened to monochrome strips, their shapes bleeding into each other, like the stipple of moonlight on water.

Alone in the deepening night, Malachi had the same feeling he got when he stood at the edge of the sea. Of something timeless, vast and enduring, full of secrets and mystery and life. With its hushed breath, hidden waters and ancient trees, the forest was a spellbound place. If there was adventure and magic to be found, this was where. Yet somehow he'd failed to find it.

If only his father had been with him. But Dad would be sick with worry by now, trying to find out where he'd gone. Malachi felt stricken with remorse. Dad was already so worn and sad, the last thing he needed was a runaway son.

His disappointments, the shifting trees, piglet's snores; they all made Malachi drowsy. He slid further down against the cage and closed his eyes. He was drifting across the threshold of sleep, to that place where thoughts flit through like moths and can no longer be made to stay, when the fourth surprising sound of the evening brought him abruptly awake.

"What was that?" he said.

He waited, then heard it again – a fluting call that repeated eerily through the bush, and from further off, a fainter echoing cry. Kiwi!

With a sigh, Malachi got to his feet. "Better finish the job, aye piggy. Might as well get that part right."

Behind him, piglet shifted and snored.

Chapter thirty-six

MALACHI MADE HIS WAY slowly back through the dark forest to the cave. His torch was dimming. He would have to work fast.

The cave was noisier now than it had been during the day. The night animals were awake and scuffling around their cages and boxes, looking for a way out. Malachi stepped around the box he'd shifted earlier and crouched next to the kiwi cages at the back.

"You guys must be hungry," he said. "Don't

worry. You'll be out in a sec."

This time, Malachi used his pocket knife's tweezers, sliding their thin blades into the first lock. After several minutes of jiggling and twisting, the padlock sprung open. Malachi reached cautiously into the cage and lifted out a large kiwi. Despite being fluffed up with alarm, the bird felt surprisingly fragile and fine-boned in his hands. Malachi held himself well clear of its feet and beak, though, as he carried it towards the entrance of the cave.

"There you are," he said. "Go get something to eat."

The second cage was quicker, but the kiwi it contained, a much smaller one, did not want to be handled. Malachi ended up prodding it with his toe towards the cave entrance and out into the night.

The third cage contained two kiwi. As Malachi crouched at the cave entrance, releasing the second, he saw something flickering amongst the trees. He let the kiwi go, and watched.

The flickering was a light. It was some way off, but moving, its beams coming and going as they passed between the trees.

Malachi turned off his own torch. Who, other than himself, would be in the forest at night? Was it the police, returning to gather evidence? Or Blacko, coming to collect the remaining animals now that the coast was clear? Malachi didn't fancy an encounter with either.

The light was heading his way. Quickly, he crept to the back of the cave, tucking himself in behind the stack of cages he had emptied earlier that day. Hopefully whoever it was would pass the cave, and him, by.

No such luck. The light grew stronger and stronger, until the forest outside the cave was alive with dancing shadows. The light swung, then stopped, right in the cave entrance.

Malachi held his breath. All he could see was the bright storm lantern, and beyond it, the dense shape of a man. The man moved closer, until his broad bulk filled the cave mouth.

At first, Malachi thought Mr Dobbs had returned. But how could he have, when only a short while ago Malachi had seen the police driving him away? Then the man lifted the lantern and Malachi saw a flash of scarlet and, clutched in the man's other hand, a long sword-shaped object. Malachi's head reeled and he pressed himself further back into the rock wall.

The man bent low and shuffled towards him. The lantern illuminated the cave like a floodlight. Whoever it was must have seen him by now. Then the person spoke. But it was a woman's, not a man's voice, and despite his perilous situation, Malachi breathed out hard in relief.

"You may as well come out." The woman's voice was oddly familiar. "I don't know what you're doing here, but I saw your light and I can see you hiding now."

The woman set her lantern on the floor. Unsure what else he could do, Malachi stepped slowly forward into the bright circle it cast in the centre of the cave.

"Malachi!" said the woman. "What on earth are you doing here?"

Mrs Green? Malachi struggled to make out the woman's face beyond the brightness of the light. Then she too stepped into the circle.

"You're the last person I expected to see," Mrs Green said.

Malachi gulped. "I know the feeling."

Malachi and Mrs Green stared at each other for a few moments. Mrs Green was wearing her crimson puffer jacket, done up against the night. It made her look twice her usual size. The sword-shaped thing she was carrying was a crow bar.

"I've come to free the animals," said Mrs

Green, lifting the crow bar. "I went to fetch this."

"That's what I was doing," said Malachi. "There's still three kiwi and the boxes to go."

"Then I'll give you a hand," said Mrs Green. "If we work together, it won't take long."

Chapter thirty-seven

IT WAS NEARLY MIDNIGHT by the time Malachi and Mrs Green had freed all the animals from their cages.

The remaining kiwi were easy. Mrs Green turned the lantern to low and, with a little coaxing, they shuffled readily from their cages, heading instinctively for the cave mouth and the forest beyond. The lizards, too, scuttled from their boxes as soon as the lids were lifted, disappearing into the dark crannies of the cave.

It was the snails that took the longest. There were more than twenty of them, crawling over the boxes' sides, or clinging to the lids and floors. Their shells ranged from coin to biscuit sized, all intricately curled and patterned, as individual as fingerprints.

Someone had thought to add a few leaves to the boxes, but Malachi could tell that they were still way too dry. The snails must be suffering, and he felt a sharp stab of anger at Mr Dobbs, Blacko and Flint.

Working quickly, they carried each snail out of the cave and found a suitable place for it in the surrounding forest. Malachi was careful to choose damp spots where there was no risk that the snails could be trodden on. His torch finally failed and he had to carry the last few snails in the dark, but he didn't mind. He was coming to love the night forest, with its furtive stirrings and secretive nocturnal lives.

At one point, while Malachi was placing

a particularly large pale snail beneath a fallen punga log, Mrs Green had come to stand behind him.

"Beautiful, aren't they?" she'd said.

Malachi could only nod in reply.

Otherwise, they'd barely spoken as they worked. When they'd finished, though, and all the cages and boxes had been double-checked for overlooked occupants, Mrs Green turned to Malachi and said, "I take it you came here with Jarrod and his father?"

Malachi nodded. "The police took them away."

"I know," said Mrs Green. "I was with them when it happened." She smiled at Malachi. "I guess you'll be needing a ride home then?"

"I guess so," said Malachi, but he didn't smile back.

Chapter thirty-eight

MALACHI SAT IN THE passenger seat of Mrs Green's car, watching her through the windscreen as she phoned his father.

Obviously she was mixed up with the Jarrods somehow. She'd admitted being with them when they were arrested and she'd known how to find the cave. Perhaps she was the one they called Blacko; a pun on her own colourful name.

Then why hadn't the police taken her too? And why had she come back to free the remaining animals? Unless Malachi's original theory was right and Mrs Green was actually the cops' stooge, here to help them evict the protestors. Either way, he should never have accepted a lift from her. He should have just said no.

They sat in silence while Mrs Green drove out of the forest. Once they hit State Highway 12 though, Malachi could contain himself no longer. "Why did you do it?" he asked in a low voice.

"What's that, Malachi?" asked Mrs Green.

"Help the police?"

"The police?" said Mrs Green. "I knew nothing about them until they turned up. I'd just happened to have found …"

"Or the council," Malachi interrupted. "Whoever it was that evicted the protestors. Why did you help them chuck the protestors out of the forest?"

Mrs Green kept her eyes on the road. "Is that

what you think happened?" she asked.

"It's that machine of yours, isn't it? Why else would the Jarrods bring it here, if you didn't have something to do with the protestors and the road?"

To Malachi's surprise, Mrs Green laughed. He'd never heard her laugh before.

"Well, you're right on one count," she said. "The machine is to do with the proposed road, but you've got me on the wrong side. I'm in the same camp as the protestors."

"You're one of them?"

"Sort of," said Mrs Green. "More on the technical side."

It turned out that Mrs Green was an environmental scientist. "I specialise in measuring and monitoring endangered eco-systems," she explained. "So we can take informed steps to mitigate damage."

Malachi might as well have been in science class for all the sense that made. "I always thought you were just a science teacher," he said.

"That's my day job," said Mrs Green. "At weekends you'll usually find me somewhere like this, working to protect the environment."

It also turned out that the protestors had not been evicted. Instead, they were at a hui in Wellington, discussing the road problem.

"The council wants to protect the environment too," said Mrs Green. "It's about finding a solution that pleases everyone."

"What if they can't?" asked Malachi.

"Then the protestors will come back. Causes like this are always a work in progress. That's why I'm installing the ecosystem monitor. To give them the data they need to back up their case."

"Is that your machine?"

"Yes, I invented it. I just hope it still works. It got a bit damaged on the journey up."

Malachi stared guiltily at his hands.

"I take it you weren't part of Jarrod's dad's smuggling ring either then," he said.

"Did you think that too?"

"I wondered."

Mrs Green laughed again. Malachi was relieved she was taking it so well. She was less straight-laced than he'd thought.

"I had no idea what they were up to until I came across the cages by accident. I heard the birds and decided to investigate."

"They were all full," said Malachi. "I opened most of them this afternoon."

"I know," said Mrs Green. "I must have found them just before you did. I went back to my car to get some tools, and got waylaid with Jarrod and his Dad. You can imagine how amazed I was when the police arrived. Was it you who phoned them?"

"I tried to, from the truck, but I didn't know where we were."

"They traced the phone." Mrs Green

glanced at him sideways. "I take it Jarrod and his father didn't know you were with them? In the truck?"

"No. I stowed away. Jarrod spotted me at the end, but I got away in the forest."

"Very adventurous," said Mrs Green. "I didn't know that about you."

"Me neither," said Malachi. "I think I'd forgotten how." He looked out the window at the passing lights. "Not that it got me very far. I came here to join the protest, but I missed all the action."

"Ah, but you tried. That counts for a lot," said Mrs Green. She was quiet for a while, then said, "It can't be much fun for Jarrod, these trips in the truck."

"It didn't look it," Malachi said. "I hope the police won't be too hard on him."

"They know he's not involved," said Mrs Green. "Still, we'll have to look after him when he gets back to school."

Malachi gave Mrs Green a weak smile. He was beginning to quite like her.

"You know your ... your ecosystem monitor," he said. "What's it for?"

"It can be calibrated for different uses," said Mrs Green. "But at Waipoua we're using it to measure the vibration and pollution that's coming off the road, and hence the potential adverse effects on the forest ecosystem if another road goes through."

Malachi gulped. Mrs Green grinned at him. "You may not have realised, but science is actually really useful. And you know the other great thing about it?"

Malachi shrugged. He doubted he'd understand it, whatever it was.

"Science teaches you to really look at things," said Mrs Green. "To examine and question and consider them. And if you can do that, if you can learn to really look at the world, then you realise that all of it is amazing, absolutely all of it. Knowing that: it keeps you awake, it keeps you alive."

Malachi nodded. "My mother used to say something like that."

"She must have been a very special woman," said Mrs Green.

Malachi looked back out the window and nodded again.

"Yes," he said. "She was."

Chapter thirty-nine

THEY STOPPED AT BOMBAY to check on piglet. Mrs Green had said they mustn't leave it, so they'd loaded its cage onto her empty trailer using the trolley she'd brought with her to shift the ecosystem monitor.

Piglet was curled up in the corner of the cage and barely opened its eyes when they shone the torch in.

In Hamilton, they stopped for hot chocolate at an all-night cafe.

"It's been so nice to have your company," Mrs Green said.

Malachi found himself nodding off over his drink. The fug and clatter of the cafe swelled and receded, so that at times it was like he was back in the truck, bouncing and swaying over endless back-country roads.

"Let's get you home," said Mrs Green, helping him to his feet.

Back in the car, Mrs Green put some music on and Malachi rested his head against the window. The next thing he knew they were slowing down, Mrs Green turned the car into a driveway and he was home.

His father was waiting on the porch. He leapt down and wrapped Malachi in an enormous hug.

"I'm so glad you're home," he said.

They helped unload piglet and thanked Mrs Green. After she'd driven off, Malachi's father crouched down next to the cage.

"What's its name?" he asked.

Malachi looked at piglet. The patch over its eye looked almost black in the dawn light.

"Ahoy Me Hearties," he said.

"Good name," said his father. "I'll call it Hearties for short." He stood up. "You know, Malachi, if you'd asked me first, I could have told you the protestors had left the forest."

"How?"

"It was in that documentary. You could have saved yourself the journey and me the stress."

Malachi tapped piglet's cage with his toe. "I wanted to go," he said. "I wanted the adventure. Even if the protestors had still been there, if I'd asked you, you wouldn't have let me go."

"I may have," his father said.

"No you wouldn't," said Malachi.

His father sighed and ran his hand through his hair. His face was pale and rumpled, like a damp shirt that has been left in the bottom of a laundry basket. "You're probably right,

I probably wouldn't have."

Malachi hung his head. So much for adventure; he would have saved them both a lot of bother if he'd stayed at home.

"You've had quite a trek," his father said. "You'd better get old Hearties here something to eat, then go to bed. It won't matter if you miss a day of school."

Malachi nodded. He certainly was tired. He picking up his backpack and headed into the house.

"Malachi," his father called. Malachi turned around. "It's really great you're back."

Chapter forty

IN HIS BEDROOM, Malachi dumped his backpack on the bed. The neck of the bottle was poking out, but he couldn't be bothered looking at it. His father was right, he needed to sleep.

The glass glistened, though, catching and holding his eye as he peeled off his socks and trousers. *Look at me*, it seemed to say. *I've got something to show you.*

"OK, OK," said Malachi, reaching over to pull the bottle out.

Inside the world of the ship, the sun had come out. The sea spread aquamarine blue from glass side to glass side, glittering like a sequined dress. What's more, the pirates were back. There seemed to be even more of them than before, or perhaps it just seemed that way from the gusto with which they were tackling the job of restoring the ship. There was action and activity everywhere.

All the debris of the battle had been cleared away and the deck was freshly scrubbed. Both the mast and its rigging had been fixed, and the sails lay folded on the forecastle waiting to be patched. There was still a hole in the ship's side, but a stack of wood stood ready for repairs, and a group of pirates was busy around it.

More supplies had been brought on board and piled beside the trapdoor to the hold. The skiff, laden to the gunnels, floated alongside, with red bandanna pirate at the tiller. Several other pirates hoisted nets and ropes to bring the cargo aboard.

Propped against the foremast, sat the pirate in the dirty jerkin. His arm was in a sling and he sported a bandage across one ear, but he was far from dead. Instead, he looked uncharacteristically merry as he basked in the sun, a flask of rum beside him.

High above, in the largest crow's nest, the stowaway also appeared happy to be back on board. He played a tin whistle as he lounged in the basket, while down below, the mermaid and the whale frisked together in the waves.

But what really caught Malachi's eye was the figurehead. Not only was she back, but she'd been freshly painted. Even the wear and tear that had previously pocked her surface had been smoothed and filled. Her face, hair and gown were radiant in the sunlight, and her pose had a new graciousness as she gazed over the glassy sea.

Malachi turned the bottle over to get a better

look at her face. Her expression was hopeful, as if she'd spied something bright and inviting on the horizon, and had the same tinge of merriness that he'd seen among the pirates. But there was something more significant about her that struck Malachi the most. How had he failed to notice it before? Perhaps, he hadn't known how to look. With her adventurous eyes and luminous smile, the figurehead looked a lot like his mum.

Malachi smiled. Then he noticed something that made him smile even more. As part of their repairs, the pirates had given their ship a name. On the bow, just below the figurehead, the name *Phenomenal* was painted in thick cream script.

Malachi considered getting out the ship's log. So much had happened over the past few days, he should record it while it was still fresh. Yet the urge to lie down overwhelmed him. He placed the bottle carefully on the floor, flopped on his duvet and went straight to sleep. The bottle rolled under the bed.

Chapter forty-one

MALACHI JOSTLED ALONG the footpath with the other kids on the way to school. His father had said he didn't have to go, but Malachi thought about the pirates, working hard to fix their battered ship, and thought he'd make the effort.

He'd planned to take his usual route along the beach, but when he got to the turn off, had decided to try the other way instead. He'd even walked for a while with some kids from his class.

They were chatting and laughing about their weekends. Thankfully, no one asked about his.

He didn't have science on Tuesdays, so he didn't see Mrs Green all day, although he kept an eye out for her during his breaks. Jarrod didn't turn up to any of his classes either, and Malachi found himself hoping he was OK. Otherwise his day felt just like any other. It was as if he'd never been away.

When he got home after school, he discovered that his father had made a run for piglet using an old dog collar, wire and chain. Piglet was trotting happily up and down the front garden, rooting the flowers out of their overgrown beds and making muddy patches in the lawn. It snorted when it saw Malachi, but didn't stop.

Malachi sat on the step and watched. He was surprised how happy he felt. It was less than a week since he'd sat in this same spot, yet something vital had changed.

Mrs Green was right. His journey hadn't

been a waste. Although he hadn't found what he was looking for, he'd been given something else. Adventure had been there for the taking all along, he now realised – and wonder, and amazement. It was just that to see them you had to be prepared to look. The forest had reminded him how. Now all he had to do was show his dad.

There was a good stretch of the afternoon ahead of him, though, before his father would be home. He would need to fill it somehow. He might as well check on the ship.

It took Malachi a while to find the ship in the bottle, which had rolled right under his bed in the night. Then when he did find it, he discovered it was no longer a ship in a bottle anyhow. It was just the bottle. The ship had gone.

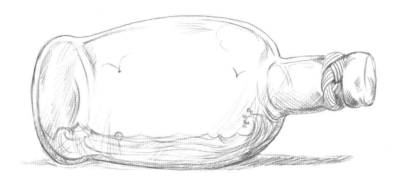

Chapter forty-two

AT FIRST, MALACHI couldn't believe it. He stared at the bottle, with its empty stretch of sea, as if the ship might return at any moment. But it had definitely gone. All that was left was a shallow hollow in the waves. Even the mermaid and the whale had disappeared.

Malachi felt as though he might cry. If he'd thought about it, he would have realised that the ship could leave the bottle. After all, if another ship could get in, then his could get out. He just hadn't expected it. He'd noticed the pirates were busy, but had assumed they were fixing the ship. He'd never considered they might leave him, never realised they might go.

A movement at the door made Malachi look up. It was his father, home from work early. Malachi hadn't heard him arrive.

His father pointed at the bottle. "What've you got there?" he asked.

"A bottle," said Malachi.

"It's a big one."

Malachi glanced at the empty bottle in his hands. He might as well tell his father all about it. It no longer mattered if he believed him or not.

"It used to have a ship in it," he said.

"Like a ship in a bottle?" his father asked.

"Yes, but the ship's gone."

"Broken?" said his father.

"Not exactly. When I found it, there was a pirate ship in it, with cannons and cutlasses and treasure – the lot. Things happened on board, and it left."

"I'm not sure I know what you mean," said his father.

"Things changed on board the ship. Sails went up and down, cargo shifted, pirates came and went. And other stuff in the bottle changed too. Sometimes it was stormy, sometimes sunny. Sometimes there were waves, big waves, then there'd be none. And there was a whale, too. It swam around."

"Really?" His father looked at the bottle resting in Malachi's hands. Without the ship in it, it looked like a large, rather weathered bottle, part-filled with a sea of sand. Even Malachi could see it would be hard to believe the bottle had ever housed a ship, let alone a fully rigged pirate ship, kitted out for battle.

"I kept a ship's log," said Malachi. "I was trying to observe the changes so I could understand them, but then the ship left."

"Can I see the log?" his father asked.

"Sure." Malachi picked up the red notebook from the floor. His father turned slowly through the log's pages, carefully reading each entry. When he got to the end, he looked up.

"You've done a good job," he said.

"Thanks."

"Thorough, I mean."

Outside Malachi's window, piglet started grunting excitedly. There were footsteps on the porch and the doorbell rang. Malachi's father handed him back the log. "I'll see who it is," he said.

Chapter forty-three

MALACHI COULD HEAR his father talking to someone on the front porch. The ship's log was lying on the bed next to him and he slipped it under his pillow. The ship was gone and he would never know where. He would tell his father he didn't want to discuss it. His father would respect that. Perhaps, over time, Malachi too would begin to doubt there had ever been anything in the bottle other than mucky grey sand.

"That was Mrs Green," his father said, when he returned. "She was wondering how you were."

"She's a nice lady," said Malachi. "I used to think she had it in for me, the way she called you all the time, but I guess she was just concerned."

"I asked her to keep an eye on you," said his father. "I was worried about you after Mum died. You seemed so lost. I guess we both were."

Malachi smiled. "So all those phone calls weren't about science?"

"Not many of them. Mrs Green had another reason for coming around just now. She thought you might be stuck for an idea for your science project. I thought you were doing it on snails?"

Malachi shifted uncomfortably on the bed. "I kind of changed my mind. I thought it wouldn't be fair on the snails, you know, taking them out of their homes."

"Mrs Green wondered if you'd like to do it on the Waipoua Forest, now that you've been there. You could cover the forest's ecology, what the protest's all about, that sort of thing. She seemed to think you were developing quite an interest in it."

Malachi nodded. "She did make it sound pretty interesting. She knows some amazing things about science."

"She also said she's going to Wellington next Friday, to the hui they're having, and she wondered if we wanted to go along – you and me. She said she'd give us a ride."

Malachi looked at his father. "What did you say?" he asked.

"I said that sounded great. If you want to go, that is?"

"Really?" said Malachi.

"Really," said his dad, laying an arm around Malachi's shoulders. "I've been thinking about what you were saying, about us never doing anything interesting. And I think you're right. I guess that in the past year, I've only felt like I can do what's easiest, and that's staying at home. It's been a way of coping with it all."

"I know, Dad," said Malachi softly.

"But things have been pretty boring around here lately, and I don't think it would do either of us any harm to have a few more adventures. So how about after we get back from Wellington we head up to this forest you're so fond of. It sounds pretty amazing and I'd like to see it. We could camp there."

Malachi couldn't stop the grin that spread across his face. "It is, Dad. It's beyond amazing. I'll make a list; I'll work out what we need to take. I can get all the stuff together, too, I know how to do it."

"That's great," said his father. "Because I reckon once we start having adventures, we're not going to want to stop."

Malachi gave his father a big squeeze. His father hugged him back.

"Speaking of adventures," said his father, "can I have a closer look at that bottle of yours?"

Malachi handed the bottle to his father, who held it up to the light coming through the window. "Pirates, did you say?" he asked.

"They flew the Jolly Roger."

"Definitely pirates then. Did their ship have a name?"

"I called it the *Bold Ship Phenomenal*."

His father looked at him. "In memory of Mum?" he asked.

"Phenomenal was one of her favourite words," said Malachi.

"I know," said his father. "And amazing and fantastic and incredible."

"And astounding and miraculous," added Malachi. They both laughed.

"Did you notice that they left something behind?" his father asked. He pointed towards the base of the bottle, where a small green ball, the size of a marble, was just visible between the crests of two waves.

"What is it?" Malachi asked.

"A buoy," his father said. "They used to make them out of glass like that."

"A marker buoy?"

"Yes. You know what that means, don't you?"

Malachi shook his head.

"That they're planning to come back. Why else would they bother to mark that spot?" Malachi's father handed him the bottle.

"There's one other thing we'll have to get sorted before we go to Wellington," he said. "We'll have to build a pen for old Hearties, before my garden's completely ruined." He stood up. "I'd better go make dinner. All this talk of adventure is making me hungry." He headed for the door, then stopped. "I almost forgot. Mrs Green brought you this."

He put his hand in his pocket and pulled something out. Balanced in the centre of his palm, was the largest snail shell Malachi had ever seen.

"Pupurangi," Malachi whispered.

"She said it's from her collection. She thought you might like it."

After his father had gone, Malachi sat staring at the beautiful snail shell in his hand. It was a rich amber colour, speckled with flecks of gold. The flecks swirled inwards and outwards like a miniature galaxy. He placed the shell next to his magnifying glass on his bedside table, then, like his father had done, picked up the bottle and raised it to the light.

At the back of the bottle, the swell parted slightly and the buoy was in clear view. His father was right; the buoy was made of glass – thick old glass, like the glass that the bottle was made from. A rope had been secured in cross-hatch pattern around it, and that rope was in turn attached to a thicker rope that disappeared down into the waves.

Malachi stepped closer to the window. At a certain angle he thought he could see something

– a shape, a shadow, an underwater shifting – in the sea below the buoy. But he couldn't be sure. With each blink, each flicker of the light, it changed. He knew better by now than to strain to make out what it was. The bottle refused to be pinned down. It would reveal itself to him when it was ready. He would just have to wait and see what emerged, what would happen next.

Placing the bottle on the table next to his bed, he reached under his pillow for the ship's log. Turning to a new page he wrote the day and date as neatly as he could in the top right-hand corner. He ruled a line under them, then shifted his pen to the space below.

Ship sailed, he wrote. *Buoy left behind. Something sunk below.*

He drew another line, then shifted his pen to the conclusions section and wrote a single word: *Treasure?*

About the author

Sarah lives with her family in Whaingaroa – Raglan, on New Zealand's wild and wonderful west coast.

The Bold Ship Phenomenal is Sarah's third book for children, and was shortlisted for the inaugural 2013 Kobo/NZ Authors E-publishing Prize.

In 2011, Sarah won the Storylines Joy Cowley Award for her picture book *Wooden Arms* (Scholastic, 2012), which is also published in te reo Māori as *Poupou Tauawhi* (Scholastic, 2012). Her chapter book, *Ella and Ob* (Scholastic, 2008) was shortlisted for the 2006 Storylines Tom Fitzgibbon Award.

When not writing, Sarah visits schools, runs workshops and attends festivals to talk about books, writing and her work.

For more information and to contact Sarah, go to: **www.sarahjohnson.co.nz**

825-8958